Jennifer Torres

the Do-Over

the DO-OVER

Jennifer Torres

Scholastic Press / New York

Library of Congress Cataloging-in-Publication Data available

ISBN 978-1-338-75419-3

10 9 8 7 6 5 4 3 2 1   22 23 24 25 26

Printed in Italy   183

First edition, April 2022

Book design by Stephanie Yang

For Alice and Soledad and every student
who kept laughing, kept learning,
kept going—and all the teachers
who supported them

1

Some catastrophes seem like they crept up on tiptoe to knock you sideways. But if you replay it all in slow motion, you'll realize you should've seen them coming. It's like, if you've ever watched old videos of figure skaters performing at the Winter Olympics. How one second a skater could be flying into a jump. The next, she's picking herself up off the ice. Just like that. But if you go back, if you watch closely, frame by frame, you'll see from the moment she took off that she wasn't going to land it.

Maybe you don't watch old figure skating videos, though.

I guess what I'm trying to say is, I probably should've seen it coming. For example, there was that week when every time someone sneezed in class, someone else would point and yell, "You have it!" Or that Friday night, when instead of streaming episodes of goofy '90s television shows like we always did, Mom made us mix a batch of homemade hand sanitizer out of aloe vera gel and some rubbing alcohol we found at the back of the bathroom cupboard.

The thing is, people say obnoxious stuff in class all the time (no offense), and Mom always has some new DIY project she wants to try. So, I didn't think it was strange at the time.

But then, after school a week later, I was waiting for my sister outside the computer lab. As usual. She was running behind. Also as usual. I was worried she was going to make me late to my skating lesson. It was a Monday, newspaper deadline day, and Raquel always has one more story to edit or one more picture to approve so the new edition of the Manzanita Mirror *can post first thing Tuesday morning.*

I was about to drag her out of the lab when my phone buzzed. It was a message from Coach J'Marie. For a moment, I was worried she was texting to ask what was taking so long, but then I tapped the message.

"Hey, Lucinda. They closed the rink. It's this new sickness that's going around. Everyone wants to be on the safe side. Looks like we have to cancel our lesson."

I had to read it twice. Not that it was confusing or anything. It was just hard to believe. See, I have this big competition coming up, the Pacific Coast Classic, and we were supposed to work on my sit spin. It was as if, one second I was on my way to practice. The next second, I wasn't. Just like that.

So, to answer your question, I guess that was the moment I realized everything had changed. But I probably should've seen it coming way before then.

Lucinda Mendoza closed her notebook, crossed "daily reflection" off her homework list, and capped her pen. She would have to type up the assignment later and upload it to Ms. King's online classroom in the folder labeled "Quarantine Diaries." But for now, her twin sister, Raquel, was hogging the laptop, meeting with the newspaper club to finish the next edition of the *Mirror*. School was closed, but it was still Monday after all.

"Ever think about taking a break, Kel?" Mom had asked earlier that morning, her voice all thick and croaky. "Considering"—she waved her arms around—"*all this*?" Mom and Lucinda had woken up to find Raquel sitting in the dark at the kitchen table, revising her latest story as she crunched a bowl of Corn Chex.

"Seriously," Lucinda added, yawning as she pulled her tangled curls into a scrunchie. "In case you didn't notice, we're in the middle of a pandemic."

Raquel swallowed and looked slowly from her mom to her sister as if she expected them to admit they were joking. When neither did, she rolled her eyes and muttered, "I'm on deadline." Then she shoveled another spoonful of Chex into her mouth and kept typing.

Eight hours later, the minute Ms. King said online school was over for the day, Raquel clicked open a new window on the laptop screen and launched the newspaper meeting. Trying to interrupt her would be pointless. So would reminding her that before Mom left for the salon, she asked them to clean the kitchen.

Instead, Lucinda nudged Crybaby, her whiny tabby, out of her lap, rolled off the couch, and took her phone to the balcony of their second-floor apartment. She needed the practice anyway.

First, she reread that message from J'Marie for what felt like the millionth time. It didn't seem possible that only a month had passed since she'd gotten it. Last month felt like *years* ago. Last month felt like it happened on another planet.

Coach J'Marie

> Hey, Lucinda. They closed the rink. It's this new sickness that's going around. Everyone wants to be on the safe side. Looks like we have to cancel our lesson.

Lucinda

> What about my sit spin? I'm still not low enough.

Coach J'Marie

> Don't panic. This is only temporary. Keep working on your off-ice exercises and stay healthy, okay?

Temporary. It was the same thing they said about schools closing, and not being able to see their friends, and wearing face masks every time they left the house.

That first weekend, when the mayor was on TV asking everyone to stay at home, Mom started yet another DIY project, making a mosaic-top table with the smashed pieces of coffee mugs they had dropped and broken over the years.

"Miren, by the time I'm done with this, everything will be back to normal," Mom reassured them.

The table was still half-finished.

I guess it figures, Lucinda thought as she set her phone on top of it. *Nothing's back to normal yet, either.* Then, resting her hands on the balcony railing for balance, she leaned forward, stretched her right leg behind her, and lifted it as high as she could. She closed her eyes and tried to imagine she was on the ice. A burst of cool air against her cheeks. Her ponytail flying. She could almost picture it. Almost. If it weren't for a sudden *bam* against the sliding glass door.

Lucinda's eyes popped open.

"In case you didn't notice, I'm *training* out here," she called over her shoulder.

Raquel cracked the door open.

"Come on, Lu, I need you inside," she said. "It's time to make story assignments for next week. Just try it out. You might like it."

Lucinda didn't budge. Ever since last summer, when Dad moved to Lockeford, five hours north in the slow, green middle of California, Raquel had been acting like she was editor in chief of their lives, not just the *Mirror*. She made color-coded schedules—blue for Lucinda, green for their mom, and purple for herself—and emailed them first thing every morning. And she was always sneaking off with Lucinda's phone to set what she insisted were friendly reminder alarms.

"She is completely out of hand," Lucinda complained when Raquel tried to teach her the *right* way to fold bath towels. "She is *editing* the laundry."

"Just . . . try to be patient," Mom said. "I think she needs to feel like there's still something she can control."

But Raquel couldn't rewrite their parents' story as if it

were one of her newspaper articles, just like she couldn't schedule Lucinda into the club, no matter how persistent she was.

"Maybe next time," Lucinda said. "Anyway, we should probably start cleaning the kitchen soon. Mom said to have it done before she gets back."

The salon was closed, like everything else. But Mom had been going in once a week to mix up dye and put together care packages with shampoos and glosses and creams for clients who were trying to keep up their color at home. You would think people had more important things to worry about than hair at a time like this, but at least Mom's new delivery service meant she wasn't worrying about money all the time like she had been at the beginning.

Lucinda tightened the sweatshirt she had tied around her waist. She took hold of the railing again and stretched her leg toward the sky.

"I remember what *else* Mom said," Raquel continued in a too-sweet singsong voice. "About you needing some *connection*, maybe a change of *scenery*."

Lucinda dropped her leg and groaned. The other night, they overheard Mom on the phone with Tía Regina.

"Marcos and I have been talking about the girls maybe going up to stay with him for a while," Mom had said, her voice low. "Kel still has her newspaper club to keep her busy. Maybe *too* busy, honestly. But I'm worried about Lucinda. She's cooped up all day and just doesn't seem to be connecting to anyone. A change of scenery might do her some good, and Marcos has all that space."

Marcos was their dad.

Maybe Lucinda did feel a little disconnected lately. But that was only because she hadn't seen her friends at the ice rink—hadn't even laced up her skates—for a month now. How could Mom think that sending her five hours *farther* away would make things any better?

And then there was Sylvia, whose face started appearing in Dad's posts right after Raquel and Lucinda went up to visit him for their twelfth birthdays last fall. They even spotted her in the background of a video chat not too long ago. Lucinda wasn't in a hurry to meet her in person.

"Mom would be *so* relieved to know you're talking to actual humans again and not just a cranky old cat," Raquel said.

"Crybaby is a sensitive soul," Lucinda protested. "And very good company."

But she had to admit that Raquel had a point. And if joining the newspaper club could convince Mom that she would be fine, exactly where she was, then it was worth a try.

"All right," Lucinda said finally. "I'm in."

2

CANCELLATIONS CONTINUE AS DISTANCE LEARNING STRETCHES INTO SECOND MONTH AT MANZANITA MIDDLE SCHOOL

By Raquel Mendoza, *Editor in Chief*

The spring production of *Xanadu Jr.* has been postponed indefinitely, sources close to the drama department tell the *Mirror.*

The cancellation comes one month after Manzanita Middle

School abruptly closed its doors amid growing public health worries.

"I haven't stopped crying since I heard," eighth grader Alice Ortega said in a video chat interview. Ortega was set to play the lead role of Kira. "We've been rehearsing for months. I even learned how to roller skate. After all that work, I can't believe we won't get the chance to perform."

The spring musical is just the latest event to be scratched off the school calendar. The basketball championship, chess tournament, and book fair have all been canceled or postponed in recent weeks.

"I understand how difficult and disappointing these decisions are," Principal Osterwald said in an email. "But the health and safety of our students is our top priority."

Osterwald did not respond when asked how long it would be until school reopens.

Raquel knew her sister would come around eventually. Still, part of her wished she hadn't brought up that phone call with Tía Regina. She saw how Lu's shoulders stiffened when she mentioned it.

"Hurry up," she said, stepping aside so Lu cou' her through the patio door. "Everyone's waiting."

Lu shook out her frazzled ponytail, then pulled it back smooth again. "I don't understand why you want me to join so badly. Don't you have enough people to boss around?"

"*Never,*" Raquel said.

She was joking, of course. Mostly. There were always more stories to write, especially now when they were "living through actual history," as Ms. King kept telling them over and over. But there was more to it than that, even if Raquel couldn't quite explain it exactly.

It was just that, when they were younger, when Mom and Dad were still together, Lu loved all the same things she did. Wanted to be wherever she was. *Listened* to her. They never dressed the same. Nothing like that. And no one ever had any trouble telling them apart. But it was as if they were connected by an invisible cord. Even if they stretched out in opposite directions every now and then, they always sprang back together.

Things started to change after Mom signed them up for

skating lessons two years ago, right after the divorce. Lucinda loved it, gliding away in a blur of brown curls and teal mittens almost from the start. Raquel, on the other hand . . . fell. A *lot*.

Thinking about that first day in skating class reminded Raquel of Ms. King's latest Quarantine Diaries question. "What was the moment you realized everything had changed?" Raquel hadn't gotten around to answering it yet. The more she thought about it, the less it made sense. The situation was *always* changing, if you were paying close enough attention. As far as Raquel was concerned, the most important question wasn't "What just happened?" It was "What happens next?"

The rink shut down. Until it opened again—and who knew when that would happen—Raquel had a chance to tug on that cord and pull her sister closer again.

She sat at the table and switched the camera back on, trying not to smile when she noticed Lu blink in surprise at the dozens of tiny windows that filled the screen. The club had more than doubled in size since school closed.

"We're back!" Raquel said. "Who has a story idea?"

Alice Ortega waved. "I do!" The background on her screen was set to an image of the stage at the Pantages Theatre in Hollywood. Her real background was too messy, she once confided to Raquel, with her little brothers around wrecking the house all day.

"Alice!" Lu said, waving back. "I didn't know you were in newspaper club."

Alice shrugged. "Now that the musical is postponed, there isn't much else to do. I mean, there's only so many times you can rearrange your bookshelves, you know?"

Raquel was adding new members to the club each week, sometimes two or three at a time, and for pretty much the same reason. The *Mirror* was one of the only activities the pandemic hadn't shut down.

"Alice is going to write movie reviews for us," she explained to Lu, then turned back to the camera. "So, what do you have planned?"

Alice's eyes widened. Her hands fluttered in front of her face. "All right. You know how we all wish we could flash forward and get to the *end* of quarantine? I was thinking it would be fun to write an article that ranks the top five movies about time travel!"

Faces inside the little windows began to nod. "Not bad," Raquel said, scribbling onto her story schedule. "I'll put you down for five hundred words. Who's next?"

"Wait," Lu interrupted, squinting at the screen. "Peter, where *are* you? Are those . . . parrots?"

There was a pause while Peter found the Unmute button.

"Cockatiels," he said. A bird bobbled on each of his shoulders. One of them lifted its head and whistled. "My parents still have to go to work. Dad's an electrician and Mom works at the pharmacy. They're essential workers. So I'm staying at my grandma's for a while."

Lu sat back in her chair and folded her arms across her chest. Crybaby jumped into her lap. "Our mom is thinking about sending us away, too," she said. "To our dad's, up in the country."

Raquel kicked her sister's leg under the table. *Stop,* she mouthed. The conversation was skidding off her agenda.

"Getting back to next week's edition," she said. "Who—"

Daisy switched her microphone on. "Wait, hasn't Kel told you our idea yet?"

"We don't really have time—" Raquel started to say.

Then Lu leaned in front of her. "No. What idea?"

Raquel felt her cheeks flush pink. "It's *nothing*! It was just a joke." And it had been. Mostly. "Anyway, we still have lots of stories to discuss, so I think we should get back to—"

Daisy talked over her, eyes glittering. "It's *not* a joke, it's a really good idea. What if you *do* go up and spend quarantine with your dad? Except instead of going alone, you bring your mom, too! It'll be just like this old movie I saw where the twins trick their parents into getting back together. Like a do-over."

Raquel felt Lu's eyes fix on her face. She fumbled with the trackpad, trying to mute Daisy before she could blab any more of what supposed to have been a private conversation. Then she froze as footsteps trudged up the stairs to their apartment.

"Mom!" Lu gasped. "The kitchen!" She leaped out of her chair, sending Crybaby sprawling to the floor with a sad whine.

Raquel spoke directly into the camera. "We have to go, guys. The meeting's adjourned, but be sure to send me those story ideas by tomorrow morning, nine a.m. sharp!" She slapped the laptop closed and bounded after Lu into the kitchen.

3

"I'll start the dishes, you take countertops," Raquel ordered. Lucinda nodded. It was one of those times she was glad to have Raquel take charge, to make a decision and run with it. They would never finish in time—Mom's key was already jiggling in the lock. But if she came home to find them *in the middle* of cleaning up, maybe she wouldn't be so upset.

Lucinda knelt and reached into the cupboard where they usually kept the cleaning spray. But the cupboard was filled, top to bottom, with rolls of toilet paper. She pulled open a drawer. More toilet paper.

"It's all toilet paper!" she whispered as Mom's keys dropped into the clay bowl on the end table near the front door.

When *all this* had started, when everyone first began to realize that the new sickness going around was something different than the usual cold or flu and that there would be long weeks stuck at home, Mom had become strangely obsessed with toilet paper. Did they have enough toilet paper? Where could they get more toilet paper? Why hadn't they stocked up on toilet paper when they still had the chance?

"How long do you think it will be before she finds a tutorial for DIY Charmin?" Lucinda had jokingly asked at dinner one night.

Mom flicked a chunk of avocado at her. "See if I share any of it with you two," she said as they giggled into their oven-baked taquitos.

Now there was toilet paper stashed everywhere. More toilet paper than Lucinda could imagine three people using in a lifetime. They could cover their walls in it, and there would still be more toilet paper. Mom had started giving it away to neighbors who were running low.

"Just . . . grab some and start scrubbing!" Raquel said through gritted teeth. Then she twisted the faucet and raised her voice over the rush of water. "We're in the kitchen, Mom! Cleaning up! Just like you said!"

Lucinda held her breath as she heard the tap of Mom's footsteps on the tile kitchen floor. She waited for Mom to ask why they hadn't finished, to ask why they had barely started, to ask . . . anything.

Raquel turned off the water and swiped her hands over the front of her jeans to dry them.

"We know you wanted the cleaning done before you got home, and we would have finished sooner, only Ms. King kept us late, and then the newspaper meeting ran over," Raquel started in that whirlwind way she had that left you too dizzy to argue. "But Lu actually came to the meeting this time, which we thought you would be happy about since you want her to make some friends, so—"

"I already *have* friends," Lucinda interrupted. "It's just that . . ."

Lucinda stopped mid-sentence. Raquel stepped aside as Mom walked silently to the sink and washed her hands. She looked as dazed as she had been that day she took Lucinda to her first skating competition and they'd been nearly swallowed by a crush of rhinestones and fleece.

"Mom?" Lucinda asked.

"Hmm? Oh! Sorry." It was as if Lucinda's voice had whisked away a cloud and Mom could finally see them again. "I . . . I just stopped to drop some groceries off for Mrs. Moreno." Mom lifted a grocery bag, then set it on the counter. A box of Raisin Bran poked out the top. "And it turns out she's sick. She has it."

"What?" Lucinda and her sister said in unison. Both of them sprang toward Mom. Raquel took one of her hands and led her to the table. Lucinda pulled out a chair.

"Thank you, mija," Mom said, sitting down. Then she repeated, "She has it."

Mrs. Moreno lived in the apartment downstairs. She checked in on them after school sometimes when Mom had late appointments at the salon, and she always brought them half a loaf of banana bread when she baked a batch. "It's too much for just one old lady," she'd say. Crybaby liked to sneak off and cry outside her door for treats.

Mom had been bringing Mrs. Moreno groceries once a week. Ever since they heard a doctor on television explain that older people should stay at home if they could.

"Will she be okay?" Raquel asked. Lucinda wanted to ask, too. But she was too afraid of the answer. She understood that the virus was real, but until that moment it hadn't *seemed* real. You couldn't see it or feel it the way you could other dangerous things. And yet, somehow, it had crept up under them.

Crybaby sprang onto Mom's lap with a yowl. She scratched behind his ears. "I think so," she said after a while. "I hope so. Her grandson is staying with her now. That's a good thing. He's the one who told me. I was so shocked I forgot to leave the groceries."

"I'll take them down," Raquel offered, reaching for the bag.

"No!" Mom and Lucinda said together. Mom put her

hand on top of Raquel's. "I'll bring it down later." Then she closed her eyes and rubbed the bridge of her nose.

Lucinda didn't move. She glanced at Raquel, who usually knew exactly what to do or say. This time, she just shook her head.

Finally, Mom opened her eyes. "You need a trim," she said to no one in particular.

The t-word. Before Lucinda fully registered what was happening, Raquel had ducked into the kitchen and turned the faucet on again. "Better get back to these dishes," she said.

Seriously? Lucinda mouthed.

Sorry, Raquel mouthed back before squeezing a drizzle of soap on a sponge.

Some people went for a long jog when they needed to clear their heads and think things through. Other people listened to music, or gardened, or painted, or sipped tea. Andrea Cruz-Mendoza cut hair. And if she didn't happen to be at the salon when she had a problem that needed untangling, she grabbed whoever was nearest. This time it was Lucinda.

"Go get a towel for over your shoulders, mija," Mom said. "I'll get my shears."

"Fine." Lucinda stomped to the hallway closet and grabbed a beach towel. Then she dragged one of the chairs to the middle of the kitchen and slouched on it.

"Thanks a *lot*," she whispered to Raquel, yanking out her scrunchie while she waited for Mom to come back with the scissors. "We had a deal. It was supposed to be *your* turn."

4

Technically, that was true. Raquel had promised Lu that the next time Mom was looking around for hair to trim, she would volunteer. It was only fair after Lu agreed to sit for an hour with her head covered in plastic wrap when Mom wanted to test out that new glaze treatment.

"Well . . ." Raquel said, tugging at the back of her hair as she scrambled to come up with an excuse. "I'm still growing out the last one."

"*Ugh.*" Lucinda rolled her eyes.

The truth was, Raquel could see that Mom wasn't

simply sorting through her jumbled thoughts this time. She was following them someplace. And if Raquel wanted to find out where, she would have to pay attention—and be ready to act—which she couldn't do if she was sitting in that chair.

A single question flashed in her mind: *What happens next?*

Mom got back from her room with scissors and a spray bottle, her black apron from the salon tied around her neck. She tousled Lu's hair, then reached into the apron pocket for a comb and some clips. "Sit up straight," she said. Lu closed her eyes and sat up taller in the chair.

Raquel hopped onto the counter and watched as Mom spritzed and combed and snipped. Her lips moved like she was having a conversation—an argument, even— that only she could hear.

Raquel leaned forward. She strained to make out bits of it.

"*Way* too close," Mom muttered, her eyebrows raised with shock.

"And for how long? ¿Quién sabe?" Her forehead wrinkled with worry.

"For the best." She pressed her lips together in a straight, sure line, the way she did whenever she had made a decision. The kind of decision she knew the twins wouldn't like.

Facts swirled in Raquel's mind, then fit themselves together like puzzle pieces. She hopped off the counter, grabbed the laptop from the table, and slipped away to the bedroom. They would have to be fast.

Silently, Raquel pushed open the bedroom door and stepped over Lu's skating bag, still packed and ready to go, as if practice could start again at any minute. The bag seemed frozen in time somehow. Like the invitation still tacked to her corkboard for a birthday party that had since been canceled. Or the packet of worksheets Ms. King sent home when everyone thought they'd be back to school two weeks later. It was as if the whole world was on pause, and they were all waiting for someone to press Play again.

Raquel pulled Lu's warm-up jacket off the desk chair

and tossed it onto her bed. She sat down and shoved aside the worksheet packets to make room for the laptop. Principal Osterwald loaned out computers when school closed, but there weren't enough to go around. Since Raquel and Lu lived together, they had to share one. She tapped the screen back to life and opened a new search window.

Her fingers flew over the keys as she listened for the sound of Lu's footsteps in the hallway. If it was just a trim, like Mom said, she should have about fifteen more minutes. Maybe twenty. That was all she needed. So when Lu poked her head in the door, exactly eighteen minutes later, Raquel was ready.

"Mom told me to come get you," Lu said, her voice wobbly, damp hair hanging over her shoulders. Feathery bits of her trimmed ends dusted her nose like freckles. "She said she needs to talk to us. Together."

Raquel nodded. "Yeah," she said. "I figured."

Lu glanced over her shoulder, then stepped through the door, Crybaby meowing behind her. She scooped him up and nuzzled her cheek against his silvery fur.

"I'm pretty sure it's because she finally decided to—"

"Send us to stay with Dad?" Raquel finished the sentence for her. "I know."

"You *know*? So what are we going to do? How are we going to get out of it?" Lu pointed to the computer screen. "Have you figured it out?"

Raquel wanted to snort but managed to swallow it back down. Mom and Lu were always accusing her of being bossy, but when they needed a plan—and even if they didn't admit it, they *always* needed a plan, especially now—who did they turn to?

She pushed the chair away from the desk and looked Lucinda in the eye, trying to steady her with her gaze. This was going to be the hardest part. "We're not going to get out of it," she said evenly.

"We can at least *try*!" Lu protested. Raquel held her finger to her lips, and Lu dropped her voice. "We have to try. What about your newspaper? What about ice skating? My competition is only six weeks away, and I haven't practiced in more than a month. What if the rink opens and I'm stuck in the middle of a farm?"

Raquel wished she could break the puzzle apart and show her sister the pieces, one at a time. Then maybe she would be able to make out the whole picture. Mom's salon was closed. The school musical was canceled. Mrs. Mendoza had gotten sick.

There was not going to be a skating competition, maybe not for a very long time. Raquel was sure of it.

But she was also sure that if she broke the news to her now, Lu wouldn't be able to hear anything else she had to say. And if the plan was going to work, she needed Lu to pay attention. To cooperate.

She turned to the computer screen. "Look, I mapped it out. Four ice rinks, all of them within an hour's drive of Lockeford."

Lu set Crybaby on the carpet. She pressed her lips together, just like Mom had done, and peered at the screen.

"If any one of them opens, you'll be ready," Raquel continued. "And I bet it'll be way less crowded than in LA. I bet you'll have the place all to yourself."

Lu frowned. "Dad wouldn't have time to take me. Not when he's trying to run the farm stand."

Raquel forced herself to take a deep breath before replying. She needed to be careful now. She tried to remember what Mom had taught her—or *tried* to teach her, anyway—about threading a needle. You had to be patient. You couldn't force it.

"Well . . ." Raquel said. "Maybe *Mom* could take you? I mean, maybe she could come with us."

Raquel realized she was lucky her sister hadn't just taken a gulp of water. She would have spit it out all over her.

"Mom?" Lu said. "No way. She'd never go for it."

Raquel knelt on the carpet so the two of them were level. "She would. If Dad asked her to come. If he told her he needed her help taking care of us, I know she'd say yes."

Lu wrinkled her nose, like she had tasted something sour. "What about . . . *Sylvia*?"

Raquel sat back on her heels and smiled. "That's the best part. If Mom comes with us, she and Dad will be forced to spend more time together, and who knows? Maybe it'll be just like Daisy said."

She knew right away she had gone too far.

Lu tilted her head and narrowed her eyes. "You can't be serious, Kel. Mom and Dad are *not* getting back together. There's no such thing as a do-over. You know that, right?"

Raquel turned away and forced a laugh. "Of *course* I know that. I don't mean *together*-together," she said. "Obviously. I just mean, it would be a chance to remind them how things used to be—how much better it used to be—when we weren't so far apart." *And if it just* happened *to turn into together-together, so much the better,* she wanted to add. She wasn't hoping for a do-over necessarily. More like a *revision,* the way you could go back and rewrite the parts of a story you didn't like.

Lu got up off the chair, crossed the room, and flopped backward onto her bed, where Crybaby was already nestled on a shaggy blue pillow. "Maybe," she said.

Finally, they were getting somewhere.

"But how do we get Dad to even invite her?" Lu asked, staring up at the ceiling.

This was her moment. Raquel stood and took Lu's

phone from the corner of the desk. "We tell *him* it's the only way Mom will let us go."

She held out the phone. "It has to come from you, though. Dad will think I'm up to something. I already typed it all out. All you have to do is press Send."

Lu sat up. "Hey, that's my phone. When did you—"

Mom called out from the kitchen, "Girls?"

Raquel shook the phone, wishing her sister would listen for once. "Just press Send."

Lucinda snatched it. Her eyes flitted as she read.

Raquel had spent so much time thinking about what to say that she knew the message by heart. It was perfect. It would work.

> I know you want us to come up and stay with you until this is over, but Mom will never let us go without her. She just doesn't want to say so because she's afraid you'll think she doesn't trust you. You have to ask her to come, too. Tell her you need her help taking care of us. Pleeeeeease?

"I would never say, '*Pleeeeeease,*'" Lu whined. "And anyway, none of this is true."

Raquel pounced on the bed, sending Crybaby skittering to the floor. "Just *send* it, Lu. Mom is going to come looking for us any second, and then it'll be too late."

Lu squeezed her eyes shut. Her finger hovered over the Send button.

"Come on, Lu," Raquel pleaded again.

At last, Lu pressed Send. With a small scream, she tossed the phone away from her as if it were charged with electricity.

Raquel picked up it up off the edge of the bed and watched the screen. A bubble appeared.

"He's typing!" Raquel whispered.

Lu clutched Raquel's wrist. "What's he saying?"

"Girls!" Mom called again, sharper this time.

Raquel hoisted herself off the bed and tossed her sister the phone. "I better go. I'll tell Mom you're changing out of the haircut clothes. That means you're going to have to deal with Dad." Then, as she was opening the door to leave, she stopped and added, "Don't blow it, Lu. *Please.*"

5

Lucinda stared at the phone, wishing Raquel hadn't left her alone with it, wondering how long she had until Mom lost her patience. Finally, after what seemed like hours, Dad's response arrived with a ping.

> Your mother has her whole life down there, corazón. And I have mine up here. She can come visit anytime, though. Every weekend if she wants. Remember, this won't last forever.

Lucinda set the phone down on her rumpled quilt and

wished she could think as quickly as her sister. The easi-est thing to do—maybe even the best thing—was to leave it there. She could tell Raquel that Dad said no. It wouldn't be a lie exactly. And maybe they'd still be able to convince Mom not to send them to Lockeford.

Yet something about the way Raquel had said "please" just now stopped her. She wasn't sure what Raquel was planning exactly, and even less sure that it would work. But Lucinda knew that, whatever it was, it was important to her. Even more important than her usual schemes and schedules. She picked up the phone again. Her fingers trembled, but she knew what she had to type. It came to her as clearly as if Raquel had whispered it in her ear.

> You have to invite her, Dad. Now. Or we won't go.

This time she didn't hesitate. (If she had, she might have talked herself out of it.) She pressed the little arrow that whisked her message off to Dad with a soft *whoosh*.

There was no taking it back now. She turned the phone facedown, climbed off the bed, and pulled a fresh T-shirt from her dresser. Partly because changing out of the haircut clothes was supposed to be her excuse for staying behind in the bedroom to begin with. But it was also because she needed an extra minute for her heart to stop thumping.

"All right, let's go," she told Crybaby after one last look in the mirror. "We can't put it off any longer." Crybaby meowed in reply and followed her down the hall.

Mom and Raquel were sitting on the living room sofa. Lucinda couldn't decide whose gaze she wanted to avoid more, so she kept her eyes on the carpet.

"There you are," Mom said. "I was about to send a search and rescue team."

"Sorry," Lucinda mumbled. "I got a little distracted."

"That's okay," Mom said, her voice softening. "I think we're all a little distracted right now." She patted the spot next to her on the sofa. "Sit down. There's something I want to talk to you about. Both of you."

Lucinda hesitated. In her experience, conversations that started like that never ended well. Maybe they were too late after all. Mom was about to send them to

Lockeford. On their own. Raquel sensed it, too. She jumped off the couch.

"Wait, Mom, before you say anything—"

Just then, Mom's phone rang. Raquel's mouth snapped shut as Mom pulled the phone from her pocket and glanced down at the screen. "Huh. I need to answer this. You two just . . . don't go anywhere, all right?" She carried the phone outside and slid the patio door closed behind her.

"Do you think it's him?" Lucinda asked.

"It better be," Raquel said.

They stayed on their feet, watching as Mom paced the balcony. She stopped and looked back at them for a moment, then turned away again and stared out into the evening.

"What did you tell him, anyway?" Raquel whispered, perching on one of the sofa's arms. "You didn't back down, did you?"

Lucinda shook her head. "No! I told him exactly what you said. That it was the only way we'd come."

They were silent after that, watching the patio door

until Mom opened it again a few minutes later. She looked from Lucinda to Raquel, then took a deep breath.

"That was your dad," she said. Lucinda leaned forward. Raquel stood.

"And we've decided—both of us—that it would be best if you two stay with him for a while. Until all this settles down."

"But—" Raquel protested.

Mom held up a hand to shush her. "I know this is a big change—for *all* of us—so we've agreed that I'll come up, too," she continued. "Just for a week. To help everyone settle in."

She paused as if she expected them to argue and looked surprised when they didn't. They were too busy trying to communicate with each other using just their eyebrows— and without Mom noticing. "All right, then. Well, I need to organize, and you two should think about getting packed."

She walked back to her bedroom.

"Only a week," Lucinda said when the door shut.

"That's long enough," Raquel said, a new plan already

whirring behind her eyes. "Just watch. Once we're together again, Mom won't want to leave."

Five days later, Lucinda was sitting in the back seat of Mom's stuffed hatchback. She rolled down the window and let the wind whip her hair into her face. When she was little, she used to dread the drive up to Lockeford. All those hours in the car, listening to Dad and Mom sing along to country radio and watching row after row of grape vines and orange trees zip by along Interstate 5. The past four weeks had been kind of like one of those car rides, she thought. Stuck inside with Raquel, wondering how long it would be until they finally got where they were going.

Crybaby whined from his carrier in the back.

"Seriously, Lu, can't you keep him quiet?" Raquel grumbled groggily. "I'm trying to take a nap."

Lucinda reached behind her and scratched Crybaby's neck. "He's just lonely," she said. "I'm sure he'd settle down if I could hold him."

Mom looked into the rearview mirror and raised her

eyebrows. "The last thing I need is that cat loose in the car while I'm trying to drive. Leave him in the carrier. He'll survive."

Lucinda didn't argue. Mom hadn't wanted to bring Crybaby along to begin with, on account of Dad's allergies. In fact, it had almost seemed easier to convince her to come to Lockeford than to convince her to let Crybaby come, too.

Miiiiaaauarr, he pleaded again.

"Arrrgh," Raquel growled, covering her ears with her hands.

Mom sighed. "Maybe we should break for lunch," she said. She steered the car off the freeway and into a gas station parking lot.

Raquel had checked road and weather conditions the night before. None of the rest stops were open. All their favorite restaurants along the way were closed, too. So Mom threw together a picnic lunch while she cleaned out the refrigerator.

Lucinda wrinkled her nose as she unpacked the cooler. "Peanut butter and jelly *burritos*?"

"I didn't want the tortillas to go to waste," Mom said as she unscrewed the top of their water bottle. She took a long gulp. "There's half a container of hummus in there, too. Oh! And leftover enchiladas from the other night."

Lucinda found a bunch of grapes and popped one in her mouth. Then she unlatched Crybaby's carrier and snuck him a nibble of string cheese.

Mom opened the trunk, and they sat side by side, their legs dangling over the back bumper as they chewed.

Raquel swallowed a bite of carrot stick dipped in pesto. "Remember that picnic at the ranchette, when you told us to pick a bouquet—"

"And we brought back a bunch of poison oak?" Lucinda finished.

Mom shuddered. "*Uf.* Unfortunate," she said. "But at least your dad's carnitas made up for it. I've missed that dish."

Raquel nudged Lucinda's shoulder. She didn't have to. Lucinda heard it, too. Mom said she missed Dad's cooking. It would have been better if she said she missed *Dad*. But, still. It was better than nothing.

Mom dusted crumbs off her lap and started to wad her trash into a ball. "¿Qué creen? Should we get back on the road?"

Raquel hopped off the back of the car. "Wait! Hold on." She pulled her phone from her pocket. "Say *carnitas*," she said.

They were still smiling, two hours later, when Mom turned onto Dad's long gravel driveway off Highway 88. Soft pink blossoms, like clouds of cotton candy, had already started to burst on the branches of the cherry trees that lined either side. Lucinda felt the same rush of excitement she always did when they got to the ranchette.

Then she noticed a red sports car parked under one of the old oak trees that towered over the property. Raquel rolled down her window and leaned out. She saw it, too.

6

It doesn't belong. That was the first thought that came to Raquel's mind when she saw the gleaming red convertible parked outside Dad's house, looking like a candy apple next to the old potato that was Dad's brown truck.

A car like that would get stuck in the mud that was everywhere at the ranchette. It would get covered in dust when they pruned the citrus trees. It would be no help with hauling. It certainly couldn't tow anything. Raquel's eyes raced over every detail. There was a sticker in the back window that said LOCKEFORD TRACK AND FIELD.

Maybe the car belonged to one of the high school students who sometimes helped at the farm stand? But that didn't make sense. Dad wouldn't have high schoolers at the ranchette right now. It wouldn't be safe. Plus, there was the necklace dangling from the rearview mirror, made of rainbow-painted macaroni noodles like the ones she and Lu had brought home from preschool.

"Did . . . Dad get a new car?" Raquel asked finally, turning to Mom for answers.

"Hmm," Mom said, gazing at the car. Her expression gave nothing away. She didn't seem concerned or even interested really. "You'll have to ask him about it."

Then she took a bottle of hand sanitizer out of the cup holder and squirted some into her palm. "Well, looks like we made it," she said, passing the bottle to Raquel. "Let's sanitize and then unload? ¿Qué creen?"

What did she think? Raquel couldn't say. Questions about the car—or to be more specific, whose it was— nagged her. But if Mom knew the answers, she obviously wasn't going to tell them. So Raquel rubbed the sanitizer gel over her hands, nudged the door open with her shoulder, stepped out, and stretched.

Lu got out next and stretched, too, bending so far forward her head nearly grazed the ground. "Show-off," Raquel muttered. Lu rolled back up and smirked, then spun around to the other side of the car to open the trunk and let Crybaby out.

"Come here, handsome," she said in a baby-talk voice as she pulled Crybaby from the carrier and held him against her cheek.

"You better be careful not to let him get out," Mom warned. "This isn't the apartment complex. If Crybaby roams around here, he's going to run into a raccoon—or, worse, a coyote. And they won't be carrying treats like Mrs. Moreno."

Crybaby purred happily as Lucinda scratched behind his ears as she slipped him back in the carrier. "You won't get out, will you?" she said, then looked up when the screen door clattered. "Dad!"

He bounded down the front-porch steps to greet them. "There you are!"

Raquel glanced sideways at Mom. This time her face wasn't so unreadable. She looked relaxed. She looked *relieved.* "Here we are." Mom smiled and took a step toward him. For a moment, it looked like they were about to hug.

Instead, Dad held out his elbow to her.

Mom just looked at it, confused for a second, then bumped it with hers and chuckled awkwardly.

Lu cringed. "Oh, geez," she muttered, shielding her eyes with her hand. But Raquel was too happy to be embarrassed for them.

Dad pulled off his baseball cap—still the LA Dodgers, Raquel noted, even this far from home—and swiped a hand through his brown-black hair. Then, turning toward the girls, he grinned. "I missed you." He pulled them into a hug, Lucinda under one arm, Raquel under the other. It was the same hug he used to save for when they came home from school. That's exactly what it felt like, too. Coming home. Like the four of them had finally snapped back together.

Dad jumped when the screen clattered open again.

"Are they here? Why didn't you tell me?"

Dad gave their shoulders a squeeze, then turned toward the woman standing at the top of the steps. Lucinda scowled. Mom's face was a mask again. She didn't look surprised. In fact, she seemed to be expecting this. She wiped her hands on her leggings and walked toward the woman, her arm outstretched. "Sylvia, isn't it?"

Then she pulled her arm back. "Sorry. I guess we're not supposed to be shaking hands right now. Anyway, it's nice to finally meet you."

Sylvia.

Her hair was swept off her face except for a few curls that fell gently over her warm brown cheeks and caught the light so that it looked like a ray of sunshine followed wherever she went. She wore rose-colored joggers and a matching sweatshirt that Raquel doubted had ever actually touched any sweat.

"Andrea!" Sylvia beamed and skipped down the steps and right toward Mom. "It's fine! After all, we're practically a pod now." She threw her arms around Mom's shoulders.

"Oh!" Mom laughed again and patted Sylvia's back.

Dad exhaled as if the worst was over. The way you do after the nurse has finished giving you a flu shot, Raquel thought. Even though your arm always ended up feeling sore and bruised later.

Lu edged closer to Raquel and stared at her with wide eyes that asked, *What is* she *doing here?*

Raquel shook her head, enough for Lu to see, but not anyone else. As carefully as she had tried to plot exactly what would happen next, she wasn't expecting this.

She needed answers. "Dad?" Raquel asked.

Sylvia let go of Mom and faced them. It seemed impossible, but somehow her smile grew even wider and more dazzling than it had been before. Lu took a half step backward as Sylvia stepped closer.

"I *cannot* tell you how excited I am to finally meet you two," she chirped. "I haven't been able to sit still all morning, isn't that right, Marcos?"

"All morning and half of yesterday," he said. His eyes crinkled at the edges when he smiled.

Raquel stared at them. "Um, what's going on?"

Mom straightened the bandanna tied around her

windblown hair and went back to the trunk to continue unpacking.

Sylvia's smile seemed to droop, but only for a moment. She slapped her palm against her forehead. "Where are my manners? It's just that your dad has told me so much about you over the past few months that I feel like I know you already. I'm Sylvia." She took Raquel's hands. "And you must be Kel."

"Raquel," she answered stiffly, and pulled her hands away.

"And you're Lucinda. But who is this?"

Mom had set Crybaby's carrier on the ground. "May I?" Sylvia asked.

"Uh . . ." Lucinda searched their faces like she was back in Ms. King's class and didn't know the right answer. "Okay?"

Sylvia unlatched the carrier and lifted Crybaby to her chest. He purred gratefully.

Traitor, Raquel thought.

"What a sweetheart," Sylvia said as she smoothed the fur on his back. "Marcos, I told you we needed an animal in the house, with all this space." She looked up at Lucinda and Raquel, and arched her eyebrow as if the three of them were in on a scheme. "Maybe having Crybaby around will convince him."

Raquel took Crybaby from Sylvia's arms and handed him to Lucinda. "So, you're ... visiting?" she asked. "I thought we were supposed to minimize contact with people who *aren't* family."

Sylvia took hold of Dad's arm and bobbed excitedly on the tips of her toes. "Tell them, Marcos."

Dad cleared his throat. "Well ... girls, Sylvia is ... well, she's—"

"I'll be staying here, too!" Sylvia interrupted. "And look who's back from her run. Perfect timing, honey!" She waved at someone behind them.

"This is Juliette," Sylvia said. "She's in sixth grade, too, and you're all going to love each other, I know it." Gently, she set her hand on Raquel's shoulder. "So you don't have to worry. We're going to be *just* like family."

7

Raquel

Hey, everyone. I wanted to let you know that we made it to Lockeford. And just because we're out of town, that doesn't mean the *Mirror* can't publish ON TIME. We'll meet on Monday afternoon as usual.

Lu

Why am I on this thread???

Raquel

You're part of the club now. Remember???

Daisy

OMG you're in Lockeford? Have your parents seen each other yet? Tell us EVERYTHING!

No one moved.

Raquel's eyes darted from Dad to Mom to Sylvia and back again as she tried to make sense of it all.

Lucinda couldn't help but feel a little sorry for her. Raquel was always so sure she had thought of every last detail. Not this time. She seemed knocked off balance, struggling to steady herself the way she had before she quit ice skating. Lucinda wanted to rush over to her the way she had back then, to offer her an arm to lean on. But Raquel would probably turn it down, just like she always did. She preferred to figure things out on her own.

Finally, Juliette stopped twirling the end of her auburn ponytail and said, "Okay, well, I guess I'm gonna go in and get cleaned up now. It was good to meet . . . all of you." Lucinda felt a little sorry for her, too, honestly. To come back from a run and find a whole new family on your doorstep.

On the other hand, Lucinda thought, except for the run, wasn't that pretty much exactly what had just happened to her and Raquel?

Then, when the door shut, the questions that had been bubbling behind Raquel's eyes spilled over all at once.

"Mom, did you know about this?" she burst.

Mom leaned against the side of the car. She tilted her head. "Of course I knew," she said. "Your dad wouldn't keep something like this from me. You know we've always been honest with each other."

Lucinda swallowed hard, wondering if Mom knew more about their plan than she was letting on. But Raquel didn't back down. "You're just not honest with *us*, though?"

"I asked her not to tell you," Dad said. "I knew it would be . . . an adjustment, and I didn't want you worrying about it. Plus, nothing was final."

Sylvia nodded. "Jules and I only moved in three days ago."

Before Raquel could respond, Mom heaved her bag onto her shoulder. "Kel, why don't you help me carry my things to the loft? We can talk about it on the walk over."

The loft? It was Lucinda's turn to erupt. "You're not staying in the house with us?" She glowered at Dad. "Why are you making her stay in the loft?"

The loft was a one-bedroom apartment above the barn at the far end of the ranchette. Dad lived there when he was in college, and after he moved out, Abuelita turned it into her sewing room. More recently, ever since their grandparents went to live with Tía Marcela in Sacramento, Lucinda and Raquel and their cousins used it for slumber parties when they visited in the summer. Lucinda loved the loft. But Mom was supposed to be staying with *them*. Hadn't that been the whole point of coming up here?

Dad started to open his mouth, but no words came out.

"It was *my* decision to stay in the apartment," Mom answered instead. "The house is going to be a little cramped with all of you living there. And anyway, I've been dying to get my hands on your grandmother's old sewing machine again. It's still up there, isn't it?"

"Right where you left it," Dad said. He seemed grateful to answer an easy question for once. "Everything's all set up. Do you need some help with the bags? Or I could drive you over in the truck?"

Mom shook her head. "I've been sitting for hours. A walk sounds wonderful right now. I'll see you later."

Lucinda's heart raced. Mom couldn't really be leaving them there, could she?

"Wait!" Sylvia said, tucking a curl behind her ear. "Don't go just yet. You must be exhausted. Why don't you come inside to freshen up? That bathroom in the loft is a little . . . rustic."

"I remember," Mom said. When Sylvia blushed, Mom added quickly, "Now that you mention it, though, it would be nice to rinse some of this dust off. If you really don't mind?"

It all felt upside down. Mom asking permission to use *their* bathroom? And yet the adults kept going along with it, as though everything were completely normal.

"Go right ahead," Sylvia said, leading Mom inside. "And afterward, we'll have a big family dinner. That way we can all get to know one another. There will be plenty of time to move you into the loft after."

"That sounds really nice, actually. Thank you for—"

Before Mom could finish, Raquel grabbed hold of Dad's arm. "I just had the best idea!"

"Whoa," Dad said, rocking backward on his foot to avoid tipping over. Raquel's eyes weren't dark and angry anymore. Now they glittered. Lucinda recognized the look. Her sister had a new plan.

"You should make carnitas!" she said. "Me and Lu will go pick some oranges just like we used to. You know it tastes better with fresh oranges."

Dad laughed. "We don't have all the ingredients. Besides, Sylvia has dinner planned already."

"Please?" Raquel insisted. "It's been too long, and Mom was just saying how much she missed your cooking."

Lucinda couldn't believe her sister had just said that. She wished she could take Crybaby and hide back in the car.

Mom shot her a warning look. "Raquel!"

"What?" Raquel said. "You *did*!"

Mom sighed. "I'm going inside. You two finish unpacking."

Raquel turned to Dad again. "Come on. Please?"

"Another time, mijita. Do what your mom said."

Sylvia linked her arm through his, and Lucinda's stomach tightened. "Carnitas?" she asked as they followed Mom into the house. "I didn't even know you could cook."

Once they were inside, Lucinda buried her nose in Crybaby's fur. "This was a huge mistake," she said.

"No," Raquel said, staring at the door. "It's even better than we planned."

8

There were times when Lu was on the ice and she'd get to spinning so fast, around and around, Raquel imagined she might keep turning forever, driven by her own momentum. That's what she worried about now. That if she let Lu's thoughts spin in the wrong direction, it would be impossible to turn them around.

"How can you *possibly* say this is better?" Lu demanded, her cheeks red. Crybaby whined in her arms. "This is worse than we ever could have imagined. We're stuck here with *Sylvia* while Mom is going to be living in the barn. How are we supposed to bring her and Dad closer together? I knew we should've stayed in LA."

Raquel grabbed Lu by the elbow and pulled her around toward the back of the car. The trunk was still open. "Shhh," Raquel said. "Everyone's going to hear you." When she was sure Lu wasn't going to start hollering again, she took Crybaby and set him on top of the stack of pillows they had brought from the apartment. Then she reached back farther into the trunk for one of her reporter's notebooks and a new rollerball pen. On the day before school closed, she raided the *Manzanita Mirror* supply closet. Who knew how much news might break before they got back again? They were living through the first global pandemic in a century. She needed to be prepared.

"Didn't you hear what happened when I asked Dad about making carnitas?" Raquel asked.

Lu slouched at the edge of the trunk, elbows on her knees. "Dad told you no," she said. "He said *Sylvia* already had something planned."

Raquel plopped down beside her. The car rocked. Crybaby lifted his head and whined.

"No." She shook her head impatiently. "I mean *after* that." The words wanted to fly out of her mouth, but she forced herself to hold them back. She needed to help Lu follow the facts along with her. She flipped to the first page in the notebook, scribbled out a sentence, and held it out to Lu.

"'I didn't even know you could cook,'" Lu read aloud. She wrinkled her nose. "So?"

"So, he's never cooked for her. He's never made her carnitas, his signature dish. Mom's favorite."

Lu shrugged. "Maybe she's a vegetarian."

"Or *maybe*," Raquel said, jumping out of the trunk, "they're not as close as they seem. Maybe he doesn't like her enough for carnitas. You heard what Sylvia said. They've only been here a few days." She started unloading the packs of toilet paper Mom had insisted on bringing along with them in case Dad's stash wasn't big enough. Raquel suspected that what Mom really wanted was to find another place to store it all. At least they had convinced her to toss out the sourdough starter before they left.

Next, Raquel pulled out a garment bag and started to lay it on the ground.

"Be careful with that!" Lu said. "It's my skating dress. The competition is coming up, remember?"

Raquel didn't want to argue with her. Not now. "I remember," she said, and gently draped the bag on top of the toilet paper rolls. "Help me with the cat food."

Lu scooted off the back of the car, and together they heaved the fifty-pound bag of cat food onto the gravel.

"Why does it matter *when* Sylvia moved in?" Lu asked. "She's here now."

Raquel pulled out Lu's exercise equipment—a jump rope, a rolled-up yoga mat, two five-pound weights, and some kind of giant rubber band. Mom and Lu just loved to tease her over how strict she was about deadlines. And yet no one ever bothered Lu about her own stubborn commitment to her fitness routine.

Finally, she uncovered her suitcase. She unzipped it to make sure the laptop was still intact and that her family-size box of Corn Chex hadn't gotten too crushed on the road. Of course she knew there were grocery stores in Lockeford and she didn't have to travel with her own breakfast cereal. But it was her secret-weapon writing fuel, and she felt better knowing she had it with her. She re-zipped the suitcase and placed it on the ground.

"I know it's not what we planned," she said, "but just think. Now we have the chance to observe Sylvia. Get to know her weaknesses. That way, if Dad doesn't decide on his own to make her leave, *we* can make sure she doesn't want to stay."

A footstep crunched on the gravel behind them.

Raquel gasped.

Lu bit her lip.

They both turned around.

9

Juliette stared back at them, raising her fingers in an awkward wave. Lucinda clapped a hand over her mouth, but it was too late to take back what they had just said. How long was Juliette standing there? What did she hear? Most importantly, was she going to tell their parents?

Lucinda shot a panicked look at her sister, but Raquel hadn't taken her eyes off Juliette. She put a hand on her hip. "It's Juliette, right?" she said. "Are you spying on us now? Well, there's no need. We haven't said anything we wouldn't say to your face."

It was harsh. Even for Raquel, who was never shy about expressing her opinions. Lucinda crossed her arms tight over her chest, not sure what to say or even where to look.

Juliette kicked at the gravel. "Relax," she said. "I only came out here because my mom told me to help you guys unload." She raised her eyes to the top of the oak tree where barn owls sometimes roosted. Not that she would know that. "I think she want us to be . . . friends, or something. And the thing is, once my mom gets an idea in her head, it's impossible to talk her out of it. So here I am."

Sylvia sounded *almost* a little like Raquel, Lucinda thought. Though she never would have said it aloud. She regretted even *thinking* it, half-worried her sister might be able to read her mind.

"Well, we don't need your help," Raquel snapped. "We were doing just fine without you—*or* your mom."

Lucinda cringed. The thought of yet another argument made her stomach twist into knots, and anyway, the situation wasn't exactly Juliette's fault. She looked around frantically, searching for some way to change the subject before Raquel blew up again.

She pointed at Juliette's T-shirt. It was dark green with a cartoon illustration of avocados doing jumping jacks. *Avo-cardio* was printed across the top.

"That's funny," Lucinda said. "Where'd you get it?"

"Huh?" Startled, Juliette looked down as if she had forgotten what she was wearing. "Oh, I made it," she said after a wary pause. "With this silk screen kit I have."

"DIY, huh?" Lucinda said, nodding knowingly. "Our mom is going to love you."

"Lu!" Raquel objected. But Lucinda could tell the distraction had worked. Raquel was already beginning to calm down. Her fingers had uncurled. Her jaw had relaxed. Her sister could be bossy, but she wasn't mean. Raquel took a step back and tilted her head, more curious about Juliette now than accusing.

"Listen, I don't know how much you heard," Lucinda continued. "But we didn't mean—" She stopped. What *had* they meant exactly? "It's just that we weren't expecting your mom and our dad to . . ." Her voice trailed off again. It felt like too much to explain all of a sudden.

Then again, maybe she didn't have to.

"Believe me," Juliette said. "This is not what I was expecting, either." She dug a little hole in the gravel with the tip of her running shoe.

Raquel sat down on the top of her suitcase. She leaned toward Juliette, ready for the story. Her reporter stance. Lucinda wouldn't have been surprised if she uncapped her pen and started taking notes. "So what happened?" Raquel asked.

"Mind if I sit?"

Lucinda slid over to make room for Juliette in the back of the car. Crybaby stretched his neck, let out a puny meow, and fell asleep again.

"I know this sounds bad, but when my mom's office shut down, I got a little excited that we were going to be able to spend some more time together," Juliette said. "But then Mom thought it would be best if we spent the lockdown with Marcos. We didn't want him to be alone, you know. Since no one knows how long *all this* is going to last."

Lucinda's breath caught as prickles of guilt crept up her throat. She and Raquel had started referring to everything that had happened—the school closing, the parties getting canceled, the stocking up on pasta and paper towels—as the big All This. And not once since All This started had she thought about Dad being on his own up here. She had Mom and Raquel. And Crybaby, of course, and all she had been worried about was when the rink would open. When everything would get back to normal again.

Yet, at the same time, she couldn't help but feel the way she had when she saw Sylvia take Dad's arm and lead him up the steps. Or when Mom had asked if it was all right to use the shower in the ranch house. It was like reaching into the closet for her favorite cardigan and realizing Raquel had taken it without asking again.

It was *their* job to worry about Dad—hers and Raquel's—not Sylvia's and definitely not Juliette's.

Raquel must have felt it, too. "We wouldn't have left our dad on his own," she said. "We talked to him almost every day on video chat, and anyway, we're here, aren't we?"

"Well, that's just it," Juliette said. She reached for one of the boxes of chocolate-dipped granola bars Mom had brought from home. "Can I have one?"

Lucinda nodded.

"Mom doesn't ever let us buy stuff like this," Juliette said as she unwrapped a granola bar. "Packaged, I mean."

She took a bite. "Anyway," she continued after swallowing. "After Marcos told her he wanted you two to come stay up here, Mom thought he'd need her help more than ever—two girls to take care of and the farm stand to run and everything. But now I think that if *your* mom is here, too, then . . ."

Lucinda had been tracing spirals in the dust on the bumper. She shook off her hands. ". . . Then maybe he doesn't need *your* mom to stay anymore?"

"Exactly," Juliette said. "And if she doesn't have to stay, that means *I* can go back. Some of the girls on my track team are still meeting up to train every morning. But I can't join them because it's too far to drive from way out here. Your dad kinda lives in the middle of nowhere. No offense."

"I get that," Lucinda said. And she did. She would have wanted to train too if she could.

Raquel tapped her pen against her teeth. "So, it sounds like we all want the same thing," she said. "You want to go home, and *we* want you to leave."

"Ra*quel*!" Lucinda said. Maybe it was true, but she could have been nicer about it.

"No, it's okay. She's right," Juliette said. "The thing is, I don't know how to convince Mom. I've already tried."

Lucinda swung her legs back and forth over the edge of the trunk. The faint smells of strawberry and cut grass swirled on the late-April breeze as the sun began to sink. This had always been her favorite time of day at the ranchette, when she and Raquel would climb the oak trees while Mom crocheted on the front-porch steps and they all waited for Dad to call them in for dinner.

"It's too bad you don't have someone else you can take care of," she mused. "Someone else who needs you."

"That's a great idea!" Raquel exclaimed. She turned to

Juliette. "Do you have any relatives, friends...anyone who might need your mom's help?"

"Already thought of that," Juliette said. "Mom's cousin Gabby lives on her own, and I know Mom was really worried about her. But now Gabby's moving back in with her parents, so it's too late."

Raquel stood. She shoved her notebook in her back pocket. "Maybe not," she said. "Maybe Gabby needs help packing...or...she needs a ride. Anything to get your mom out of the house for a couple of days. That's all we need. What if we send an email *pretending* to be Gabby and—"

"*Kel!*" Lucinda interrupted again. "That's a terrible idea! We can't do that."

Juliette paced between them. "You're right," she said. "It won't work. Mom will know the email address is a fake."

"Thank you," Lucinda said, grateful she finally had some back up.

Then Juliette continued, "Maybe instead I could say that Gabby called and asked me to deliver a message!"

Lucinda's mouth fell open. She couldn't believe they were actually thinking of going through with this.

The front door creaked open then, and they all went quiet. Sylvia called out from the porch, "Everything going okay out there?"

"Couldn't be better," Raquel called back.

10

Raquel chased a pea around her plate with her fork, hating to admit that she actually kind of liked the meal Sylvia had prepared. It was just that Sylvia made such a fuss over the paella, chopping onion and sautéing chorizo and grinding up spices in Abuelita's old stone molcajete. She even brought out a special pan to cook it in. "It was made in Valencia," Sylvia said as if that fact would astonish them. But it didn't look much different from a normal pan except that it was wider and had two handles and would take up way too much room in Dad's cupboards.

And in fact, the more Raquel thought about it, the paella wasn't so different—definitely wasn't *better*—than anything Mom could have made at home if she had the time. Even without a fancy Spanish pan and tiny vials of spices. If you took away the shrimp and sausage, it was more or less arroz con pollo, wasn't it? Same as they ate almost once a week.

Raquel looked around the table. Across from her, Lucinda was sneaking nibbles of shrimp to Crybaby, who pawed greedily at her leggings. Mom sat on the spare chair they had dragged in from the hall closet—as if *she* were the guest here—quietly chewing a giant forkful of rice. Dad swirled the ice around in his glass of water so the cubes clinked against the sides. Sylvia caught her eye and smiled, which sent Raquel's eyes back down to her plate. They had already talked about the drive (it had been fine, no traffic), about the weather (cool for this time of year), about the pandemic (what a strange time to be living through; no one could believe it was happening). Raquel was losing patience. She and Lu—and Juliette, if they could really trust her—needed to come up with a plan to get Sylvia out of the house. The longer she stayed, the harder it would be.

"Your allergies don't seem to be acting up, Marcos," Mom said after a while. "Springtime used to be so hard on you. Are you taking something new?"

Dad was still chewing, and before he could swallow, Sylvia put her fork down and answered for him.

"Local pollen," she said excitedly. "The idea is that by taking a spoonful a day, you can expose your immune system to small doses of the allergens in the air. Over time, you lose your sensitivity to them."

Raquel cleared her throat. She had read about this once. "Actually, there isn't much evidence that—"

"I figured it couldn't hurt," Dad said, talking over her.

"Couldn't hurt?" Sylvia said. "I swear by it." She leaned toward Mom. "I've been trying to tell him he should start stocking it at the farm stand. Along with some artisanal soaps and maybe specialty preserves from some of the local growers. It would bring in an entirely new customer base, don't you think?"

"What's wrong with our old customers?" Raquel tried

to break in again. It had been mostly neighbors who shopped at the farm stand, and tourists heading east into the Sierra Nevada or west toward the vineyards and the ocean beyond them. A famous chef from Sacramento came once a week for fresh produce. The *Lockeford-Clements Gazette* had even written a front-page story all about it. Abuelita had saved the clipping and framed it at the farm stand. Why did they need *new* customers all of a sudden?

But Mom sent Raquel a warning glance, so she didn't press it any further. She just went back to pushing peas around her plate.

"Well, it sounds like you're taking things in some exciting new directions," Mom said, smiling.

Sylvia nodded. "We don't want it to be Lockeford's best-kept secret anymore, do we?" She squeezed Dad's hand.

One word stood out to Raquel. *We.* Not only had Sylvia taken Mom's place at the table, but now she was talking about the farm stand as if it were hers? Raquel pushed her plate away. "May I be excused? I need to work on a story."

"You've hardly eaten," Dad said.

"I'm not hung—"

"Raquel!" Mom said. She raised an eyebrow. She didn't have to. Raquel knew Mom was serious when she used her full name.

"Fine," she muttered and shoveled up a forkful of rice and chicken.

Sylvia dabbed the edges of her mouth with a paper towel. "A newspaper story, huh?" she said. "I'd love to read it. I don't know if your dad has told you, but I work in the communications industry, too. My agency produces videos for social media. That's how your dad and I met, actually. Marcos hired us to make some videos to advertise the farm stand."

"Oh," Raquel said flatly. But Sylvia didn't seem to notice that no one—absolutely *no one*—was interested in hearing all about their love story.

"And we just hit it off, didn't we?" She gazed up at Dad. He laughed, and his cheeks turned a little red. Lucinda grimaced, and Juliette squeezed her eyes shut.

"Anyway," Sylvia said, turning back to Raquel, "I'd be

happy to show you around my office someday once *all this*"—she gestured around the room—"is over and things get back to normal again. Maybe you can even get some real-world experience."

Raquel took a sip of water and set her glass down. A little too hard, possibly. "No thanks," she said. "I'm interested in journalism. Facts. It's not the same thing as what you do."

Mom tilted her head way back and exhaled heavily. This time it was Dad's voice that was a warning. "Ra*quel*."

Sylvia pressed her hand on his again. "No, no, she's right, Marcos. My mistake. But the offer always stands in case you ever change your mind."

Everyone was quiet after that. Raquel thought the conversation was finally over. She would take a couple more bites to satisfy Dad, then find some excuse to get Juliette and Lucinda into the same room so they could figure out a way to stop this.

Instead, Sylvia kept trying to get to know them. She was definitely persistent, Raquel admitted. She had to give her that much.

"So, Lucinda," Sylvia said. "I hear you're quite the athlete."

Lu scratched Crybaby under the chin as he circled her ankles. "I guess," she said. "I haven't been able to practice much lately."

Sylvia reached to the center of the table and spooned another serving of paella onto her plate. This meal was *never* going to end. "I bet you and Jules have a lot in common. Maybe you can start jogging together. Jules can show you all the best spots."

Juliette rubbed the bridge of her nose. "She already knows the best spots. This is her house, remember?"

Sylvia frowned and put down her napkin. But it wasn't because of Juliette's tone, Raquel realized.

"Why are you rubbing your head? Is it hurting?" Sylvia asked. "You look a little pale. Do you feel all right?"

"Not really," Juliette said. Then she sneezed.

11

They all stared at Juliette as if she were a firework they had lit, about to burst into sparks and flame at any moment.

Lucinda didn't know if she should back away and take cover, or if she should try to help. Crybaby leaped onto her lap, and she was grateful that at least she had something to do with her hands now.

Juliette sneezed again.

"Okay," Mom said decisively, sliding her metal folding chair away from the table. "I'm getting the thermometer. Is it still in the bathroom cabinet?"

Dad nodded. He had gotten up to join Sylvia on the other side of Juliette.

Sylvia held her palm to Juliette's forehead and then her cheek. "You don't feel like you have a fever," she said. She turned to Dad, her forehead wrinkled with worry. "What are the symptoms again? Does your throat hurt?" she asked, holding Juliette's chin in her hands. "What about your stomach? Do you still have a sense of smell?"

Juliette sniffled. "I'm fine. Just tired." She sneezed again.

"Bless you," Lucinda said, but no one was paying attention to her.

Mom got back with the thermometer and passed it to Sylvia. It was an old-fashioned kind, with a pointed end that Juliette was supposed to hold under her tongue until it beeped. It was so quiet while they waited that Crybaby's purr sounded like the rumble of an engine.

"Maybe it's the cat," Dad suggested, his voice low. "Or the dust from running around the orchard. She could be allergic."

"Maybe." Sylvia watched the numbers slowly tick upward, then stop. The thermometer beeped.

Lucinda held her breath, remembering Mrs. Moreno. Remembering, all of a sudden, why they were at the ranchette in the first place.

"Ninety-nine point one," Sylvia announced. "That's a little high."

"Only a little," Mom said, coming back from the kitchen with a fresh glass of water. She set it in front of Sylvia. "It could be nothing."

Sylvia took a sip. "Still," she said. "I should call her doctor, just to be safe."

"Of course," Mom said. "Kel, Lucinda, help me get these dishes out of the way." They started stacking forks and plates, then followed Mom into the kitchen as Dad led Juliette to the living room couch.

Mom opened a drawer, pulled out a dish towel, and tossed it to Raquel. "You two start washing up," she said. "I'm going to see if Juliette needs anything."

Lucinda twisted on the faucet, then reached under the sink where Abuelita had always kept the soap. It was strange how so many things had stayed exactly the same for years. Maybe even decades. The drawer full of dish towels, the thermometer in the bathroom cabinet. Even the mini herb garden on the windowsill. And yet, somehow everything felt so different. It reminded Lucinda of those puzzles in the magazines they flipped through at the dentist's office. There were two pictures, side by side, that looked almost exactly alike, and you had to search for tiny differences between them.

Only in this version, there was just one difference, and she wasn't hard to spot: Sylvia. As Lucinda scrubbed burnt rice off the bottom of the paella pan, she wondered if she'd ever get used to having it in the house. To having *her* in the house. She wasn't sure she wanted to get used to it.

"Do you think she's faking?" Raquel whispered as she dried off a dinner plate. "Juliette, I mean."

They had only known Juliette a few hours, but she didn't seem like the kind of person who would lie about something so serious. "No," Lucinda said. "Do you?"

"Nah," Raquel said. "But it'd be a pretty genius idea if she was. Everyone is completely distracted."

Lucinda elbowed her in the ribs. "You shouldn't joke about it. What if she's really sick?"

She strained to hear Sylvia's phone call. "Thank you very much," she was saying. "Yes, I'll call right away if she starts feeling worse."

Lucinda turned off the water. "I think she just hung up," she whispered. Raquel wiped her hands with the towel, and they wandered back into the dining room, where Mom and Dad were already waiting.

First Sylvia studied Juliette, wedged into a corner of the sofa with a fleece blanket draped over her. Then she looked at Dad.

"The doctor thinks she's probably fine," she said.

"Thank goodness," Mom said. "That sounds promising, doesn't it?"

"But . . ." Sylvia went on.

Raquel raised her eyebrows and glanced sideways at Lucinda. *But?* she mouthed.

"Just as a precaution," Sylvia said, "she thinks Jules

should isolate for a few days. To make sure she doesn't have it."

"You mean you have to go home?" Raquel piped up. "Don't worry, we can help you pack."

Lucinda caught her sister's wrist and squeezed hard. Most of the time she admired Raquel for asking the questions everyone else was afraid to ask, for speaking up when everyone else was too shy. But once in a while—like now, for example—she didn't think it would be so terrible if Raquel were maybe a little less brave.

Fortunately, the adults weren't paying attention to anyone but Juliette.

"Can't she take a test?" Dad asked. "So you don't have to worry?"

Sylvia shook her head. "There still aren't enough tests," she said. "You can't get one unless you know for sure you've been exposed, and we don't." She brushed a strand of hair out of her face, looking tired all of a sudden. "I hate to ask, Andrea, but can Jules and I move into the apartment? Just until we know for sure?"

Mom didn't say anything for a long moment. She

looked too surprised. Then she swallowed and stammered, "Of . . . of course. Definitely. There used to be a couch, back in the den. I can camp out there. It's no problem at all."

Sylvia smiled gratefully. "And, Marcos," she said, "I know I said I'd help you at the farm stand tomorrow, but I don't think—"

Dad stopped her with a shake of his head. "Of course not," he said. "Don't worry. I'll be fine."

"And we can help," Mom added. "The girls and I. We've done it before."

Lucinda was only half listening. She knew it was wrong, but she couldn't help feeling almost . . . a little bit . . . *pleased*. As long as Juliette really was okay, this might be the opportunity they were looking for to get Sylvia out of the house. Things couldn't have worked out any better if Raquel had planned this all along.

She looked over her shoulder to see if her sister was thinking the same thing. But she wasn't there. She was in the living room, kneeling next to Juliette and jotting something in her notebook.

"Kel!" Mom and Dad spotted her a second after Lucinda did.

Raquel blinked back at them innocently. "I was just getting her phone number," she said. "So we can text each other while she's stuck in the loft."

Dad took a deep breath. "That's very thoughtful of you, Raquel, but maybe you should give Jules a little . . . space."

Raquel stood and tucked the notebook back in her pocket. Then, as she walked past Lucinda, toward the hallway that led to the bedroom they shared at the ranchette, she winked. Lucinda was excited but also a little scared. Exactly the way she always felt when Raquel had a new plan.

12

From: **Raquel**

To: **Mom, Dad, Lu**

Re: **Schedule for Sunday**

Hi, Team Mendoza! Since we're staying together now, I decided it would be easiest to make one schedule for all of us. And, Dad, I added you, too!

5:30 a.m. —Raquel wakes up (The rest of you are welcome to join me, of course.)

6:30 a.m. —Mom and Lu wake up (Seriously. **You have to get up.**)

6:35 a.m. —Breakfast and getting dressed

7:00 a.m. —Farm stand

9:00 a.m. —Back home for a snack and text/email break

10:00 a.m. —Farm chores together

12:00 p.m. —Lunch

1–4:30 p.m. —Family time (Board games? Puzzles? Home videos? Long walk? I'm open to suggestions!)

5:00 p.m. —Dinner (Carnitas?)

The sky glowed bluish-violet and birds had just begun chattering in the trees when Raquel woke up the next morning. Operation Quarantine: Day 1. She stretched her arms, then clambered down from the top bunk, careful not to step on Lu—or Crybaby, who snoozed on the pillow beside her sister's head. Raquel was used to waking up before Mom and Lu. Sometimes hours before. She had never needed an alarm clock. Something inside her mind just clicked on each morning, to tell her the world was in motion again and she wouldn't want to miss any of it.

It was always harder to beat Dad to the breakfast table, though.

Raquel found him in the dim kitchen, pouring a cup of coffee.

"I hope I didn't wake you," he said. "It's been a long time since I had to worry about making too much noise in the morning."

"No," Raquel said, and shivered. The ranch house was comfortable but old, and chilly air sneaked in under windows and doors. She pulled her sweatshirt tighter around her shoulders.

Dad took another mug from the cabinet. It had a pair of dice and a hand of playing cards on it, brought back from one of her grandparents' trips to Las Vegas. "Don't tell your mom," Dad said as he filled it halfway to the top, then added a splash of cream and a teaspoon of sugar. The coffee warmed Raquel's hands as she carried the mug over to the kitchen table and sat down.

She and Dad used to spend quiet mornings together like this all the time when she was younger, especially on weekends when Mom didn't schedule her first clients until after eleven so she could sleep in.

Dad had the newspaper delivered on Saturdays and Sundays, and as she crunched her cereal and slurped her milk, he would tell her what the weather was like all over the world. "Looks like it's going to be a foggy morning in Houston," he would say. Or, "Better bring a snowsuit if you're visiting Helsinki today." And she would giggle, knowing that if there was anything to plan, anything to schedule, Dad would take care of it. She didn't have to worry.

Mornings were lonelier since he and Mom broke up, and worse since Dad had moved up to Lockeford. That was when she missed him most, when she was the only one awake in the sleepy apartment. Mom and Lu seemed to think she got up early on purpose to work on *Manzanita Mirror* stories. But really, she started working on the stories as a way to keep her mind busy while she was all alone in the kitchen.

Not this morning, though. Raquel wished they could just sit there forever, flipping through crinkly newspaper pages together. Despite everything that had changed, this still felt exactly the same, quiet and calm. For her, anyway. She could tell Dad was getting anxious about the time. He kept looking at his watch,

"I guess your mom and sister still aren't morning people, huh?" he said after he swallowed his last drink of coffee.

They should have been up by now. Raquel set their alarms herself last night. They sometimes slept through them, though. She should have set two. This was the first chance the four of them had—*just* the four of them—to be together again, and it was already getting off to a rough start.

"I'll go get them," Raquel said, worried Dad might get impatient and decide to restock the farm stand on his own.

"We're here," Mom said groggily as she and Lu plodded into the kitchen. "We're up."

Raquel tugged the edge of Lu's long-sleeve shirt. "What took you so long?" she whispered.

"Sorry," Lu said, yawning. "It's just so early."

Dad ruffled Lu's tangled hair. "Good morning, mija." Then he rinsed his coffee mug in the sink and put on his baseball cap.

"The coffee is still warm," he said to Mom. "I made a little extra for you. I'll be outside loading up."

"We're not having any breakfast?" Mom asked.

"No time," Dad said as the door shut behind him.

Abuelito named his property Rancho Los Robles after the oak trees that had grown there for nearly one hundred years. It wasn't really a ranch. Real ranches were much bigger. It wasn't even a farm. Those had animals. It was just twelve rolling acres where Abuelito raised oranges and lemons and two kinds of cherries—bright red Bings and the creamy-pink Rainiers that were Raquel's favorite—and where he tended a sprawling garden that burst with vegetables nearly all year long.

Abuelito built the farm stand at the very edge of the property, along busy Locke Road, to sell the produce his own family didn't need. Which turned out to be a lot after a while. Now Dad kept the farm stand open Thursday through Sunday, stocking it each morning with whatever he had picked the day before. Customers paid on the honor system, dropping their money in a cash box that was bolted to the side of the shed.

"Why don't you just hire someone to do this?" Mom grumbled as she arranged bunches of carrots into bushel baskets.

"Quality control," Dad said. "Speaking of which, that carrot is bruised on top. Didn't you notice? You should toss it."

It was the third time that morning that he had criticized her sorting. Raquel wished Mom would start being more careful. She wished Dad would stop being so picky. They were supposed to be working together. Raquel wanted Dad to see that there wasn't any reason to expand the farm stand like Sylvia suggested. Let alone expand their family.

Lu seemed to be hiding from any hint of conflict. She had popped in her earbuds as soon as their parents started bickering on the short drive to the farm stand, just like she used to when they all lived together. And now she was sitting in the corner on an overturned bucket, updating the chalkboard price list. It would be up to Raquel to try to save the morning. As usual.

She passed Mom a strawberry. "You should try one," she said. "Weren't you just saying the other day how much you missed farm-fresh strawberries?"

Mom set down the bunch of carrots she was holding, took the strawberry, and bit into it. "Mmmm," she said as a droplet of juice ran down her finger.

"They're as delicious as you remember, right?" Raquel asked. "Isn't everything here as perfect as you remember?"

But before Mom could answer, Dad dropped a crate of oranges on the table in front of them. "You know, if you keep eating all the product, there won't be any left to sell," he said. Raquel couldn't tell whether he was kidding or not.

Mom threw up her arms, then grabbed an empty basket and stomped away from the shed. "I'm going to the flower beds," she said.

"For the last time, we're not selling bouquets!" Dad

called after her. "It's a farm stand, not a flower shop."

This was a disaster. Raquel had held out as long as she could. She took her phone from her pocket and typed a new message to the *Manzanita Mirror* group text.

Raquel

> I know it's the weekend, and we're not supposed to meet again until tomorrow. But I need to call an emergency brainstorming session. Today at noon! Don't be late.

Normally, she couldn't stand last-minute schedule changes. What was the point of having a schedule if you weren't going to stick to it? But, let's face it, *nothing* had gone according to schedule today.

13

It wasn't like Raquel not to have realized from the start that the morning was going to be messy. Mom was the type of person who needed her sleep, especially after such a long drive and all the commotion of the night before. Not to mention the stress of the past couple of months—the salon closing, the empty grocery store shelves, all their worry about getting sick.

And Dad had probably gotten used to doing everything his own way after living alone for almost a year now. Obviously, they'd both be prickly. Raquel was just so sure she could force them back together that she hadn't thought things through all the way.

Lucinda stretched out on the bottom bunk in the bedroom that used to belong to Dad and Tío Tony when they were growing up. There were boxes of their old comic books still stacked in the closet. Lucinda was grateful that Dad remembered to save the room for them. That he hadn't offered it to Juliette instead.

That reminded her, though. She flicked on her phone and tapped out a message.

Lucinda

Hi. It's me, Lucinda. How is everything going over there?

Raquel had shared Juliette's contact information the night before. Her reply appeared almost instantly.

Juliette

SO BORING. I'm tired of TV. I'm tired of video calls. Mom won't even let me outside to go jogging. I did get a weird message from your sister, though. Something about a daily schedule?

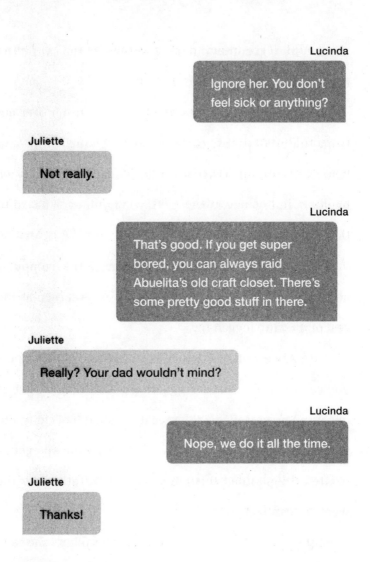

Lucinda

Ignore her. You don't feel sick or anything?

Juliette

Not really.

Lucinda

That's good. If you get super bored, you can always raid Abuelita's old craft closet. There's some pretty good stuff in there.

Juliette

Really? Your dad wouldn't mind?

Lucinda

Nope, we do it all the time.

Juliette

Thanks!

Lucinda set the phone on the bedside table. Crybaby whined, then curled up on top of her feet for a midday nap. She was tempted to take one, too. That is, until Raquel's head appeared, hanging over the edge of the top bunk. "Are you coming up here or what?" she said. "The meeting's about to start."

"I'm coming." Lucinda sighed. She eased her feet out from under Crybaby, careful not to disturb him, and hoisted herself up to the top bunk. "But I don't see why we need an emergency meeting. Haven't you ever heard of taking the weekends off?"

"Just sit," Raquel said. She balanced the computer across their laps, and they huddled over its screen as the rest of the club logged in.

"Hi!" Alice chirped nervously. "Listen, Kel, I know you're probably wondering where that movie list is because I promised you I'd have it finished by Friday, but when I told my mom what I was working on, she got so excited she planned this whole movie marathon for the weekend, and—"

Raquel clicked her microphone on. "It's okay," she said. "I forgot all about the deadline, actually."

"You did?" Alice said.

"You *did*?" Lucinda echoed. One by one the faces on the screen blinked back with the same look of wary surprise.

Since when had Raquel ever forgotten about a deadline?

"No big deal," Raquel said. "We can just publish it next week."

Lucinda couldn't believe what she was hearing. She muted their microphone, then said, "Are *you* feeling okay?" Maybe it was Raquel they should all be worried about, not Juliette.

Raquel rolled her eyes. "I'm fine." She clicked the microphone back on. "Um . . . Peter, you were raising your hand?"

Peter's face filled the screen. No cockatiels this time, Lucinda noticed. His parents must have the weekend off, at least.

"I know you didn't like my last story idea about tricks you can teach your pets during the lockdown, but I have another one I think you're really going to love."

"Go ahead," Raquel said.

Peter took a breath. "Well, I was thinking, you know how my mom and dad still have to go to work, even though almost everyone else is supposed to stay home? What if there are people who still have to work at

Manzanita Middle School? Like the janitor. I could write a story about them."

"Maybe a profile, or a day-in-the-life story," Raquel said, nodding. "That sounds great. You should definitely write that. And the pet one, too. Write whatever you want."

Whatever he wanted? Lucinda was convinced now: There was something Raquel wasn't telling her. She hadn't even looked at the schedule.

Daisy spoke up next. "So, I know this is kind of off-topic, but I just *have* to know: What's going on at your dad's house? Have you gotten your parents back together yet?"

A flurry of messages flooded the chat box.

I was wondering the same thing.

Me too!

Yeah, what's going on?

"Actually," Raquel said, "that's why I called this emergency meeting. We need your help."

Lucinda yanked away the laptop. She switched off the

microphone *and* the camera. "What are you doing?" she asked, glancing at the bedroom door to make sure it was shut tight.

Raquel yanked the laptop back. "We obviously can't do this alone. You saw what happened this morning."

She got back on-screen and told the club everything. About Sylvia, about Juliette, about that morning's fiasco at the farm stand.

Finally, she picked up a notebook and pen. "We only have a few days until Juliette is out of quarantine. Maybe less than that. I need your best ideas for getting rid of Sylvia once and for all. Who wants to go first?"

Daisy's hand shot up like a rocket. "I was hoping you would ask!" she squealed. "Okay, I've been thinking about it a *lot*, and I have the *best* idea. You have to re-create your parents' first date. It'll remind them of why they fell in love in the first place. Totally romantic."

Lucinda was skeptical. And slightly worried. "Our parents met in college," she said. "It probably wasn't that romantic. And anyway, we're not trying to get them back *together*, just bring them closer, *right, Kel*?"

"Sure," Raquel answered. She passed the computer back to Lucinda and started writing in her notebook. "But there's nothing wrong with reminiscing, is there? That's a great idea, Daisy. I'm jotting it down. Next?"

Charlie Lam, who used to be captain of the speech and debate team, raised his hand. "What if you get Sylvia up early some morning and make her spend the whole day with you, doing farm chores? Really hard ones that'll make her so miserable she wants to leave. Like cleaning out the pig sties or something?"

Raquel tapped her pen against her teeth. "No pigs," she said. "And anyway, she actually seems to like it here."

Olivia Lozano hadn't said anything during the whole meeting. Lucinda wasn't sure she was even still connected. Her internet was always cutting in and out during class. But then she asked, "Is there anything your mom is really good at? Something she can do *better* than Sylvia?"

Lucinda and Raquel looked at each other. "Not cook," Lucinda admitted. "Sylvia's paella was pretty incredible."

Raquel's eyes lit up. "I have it!" she said. "It's perfect. A haircut."

14

As soon as the meeting ended, Lucinda began winding her hair into a tight bun.

"No way," she said, snapping a scrunchie around it. "Mom just cut my hair, and after the morning we had with Dad, she's going to want to do something *creative* if she gets her hands on our heads. Plus, it's *your* turn."

She climbed down from the top bunk, riffled through her bags for a sweatshirt, and zipped it to her chin, pulling up the hood for extra protection.

Raquel closed the laptop. She sometimes wished she

didn't have to stop and explain absolutely everything. Especially when there was so little time to waste.

"Just calm down. Mom's not going to cut your hair," she said, trying to hide her impatience. "She's going to cut *Dad's*. Let's go." Not only would giving a haircut help Mom slow down and collect her thoughts, it would force her and Dad to spend the quiet time together—*close together*—that they'd been too cranky for that morning.

She jumped off the bed and headed for the bedroom door.

"Now?" Lu asked.

"The sooner, the better," Raquel said. She strode into the hallway. Sure, Raquel and Lu would have more time to prepare if they waited a few days. But Sylvia and Juliette might be back in the house by then. Mom might be packing up for Los Angeles. They could lose their chance.

"They're never going to go for it," Lu whispered, right at her heels. Crybaby trotted along after them.

Raquel paused at the doorway at the end of the hall.

Mom was at the kitchen table humming to herself and tracing rectangles onto scraps of fabric. "Leave this to me," Raquel whispered back.

She sat down across from Mom. "What are you working on?"

Mom glanced up and lifted her reading glasses to her forehead. "Face masks," she said. "I found these vintage tea towels of your abuela's in one of the cupboards. Don't you just love the patterns? Your dad said he didn't need them anymore, so I thought I'd try to do something else with them. Would you like to help?"

Raquel grimaced. "No, thanks." Even if she'd wanted to, she couldn't let herself get sucked into one of Mom's projects. She needed to stay alert so that when the right moment came, she could pounce on it. The way Crybaby stalked spiders around their apartment back home.

"I'll help!" Lu said eagerly.

"Thank you, *Lucinda*," Mom said. "I'll trace, you cut." She handed Lu her crafting scissors and a piece of fabric with a pattern of cherries and tiny blue daisies printed on it.

At least this way Lu's hands would be busy and she wouldn't start chewing her thumbnail the way she always did when she got nervous. Mom would definitely know they were up to something. For someone who liked to fling herself onto a sheet of ice, balanced on what were basically knife blades, Raquel's sister could be surprisingly cautious.

Raquel picked up the roll of elastic that Mom was using to make ear loops and stretched it. "Where's Dad? Shouldn't he be back by now?" He had gone to the vegetable garden after lunch, planning to pick snap peas to take to the farm stand the next day.

Mom unfolded another tea towel, this one covered in bumblebees, and smoothed it out in front of her. "You can go out and look for him," she said without looking up. "But my guess is he'll be back any minute . . . And stop stretching that elastic, you'll wear it out."

Raquel dropped the elastic. She got up and wandered into the living room, then sank to the carpet to work on a puzzle someone had started on the coffee table. Now that she had a plan, the waiting was unbearable. Crybaby strolled over from the kitchen table and nuzzled against her knee.

Raquel patted him lazily with one hand and, with the other, picked up a piece of what looked like a tree. Then the back door swung open.

"You're back!" Raquel jumped from the floor, scattering the puzzle pieces. Crybaby darted away with a sulky howl.

"It's nice to see you, too." Dad grinned as he pulled off his boots.

Raquel followed him into the kitchen, where he opened the refrigerator and pulled out a bottle of water. "How was the garden?" she asked.

Dad twisted off the cap and took a long drink. "The snap peas look good," he said. "Cauliflower, too." Then he leaned in. "And don't tell your smart mom, but I went back to check on the farm stand, every single one of those bouquets of hers sold."

"Heard that," Mom said, still working at the kitchen table. "You're welcome."

Raquel snuck a glance at Lu to make sure she had

heard. Lu smiled back. They were already getting along better, and it had only taken one day without Sylvia. Then, finally, Dad took off his baseball cap and ran a hand through his hair. This was it. Time to act.

"Whoa, Dad, your hair has gotten really long," Raquel said. "When was the last time you cut it?"

He jammed his hat back on. "Hey, take it easy," he said. "Everyone's hair is long right now. It's the trend. Lockdown style. You don't think it looks good?"

Mom looked up from her sewing and smirked.

"What about you, Lucinda?" he asked. "You'll stick up for me, right?"

Lu put down the scissors and looked up at Dad. She started to bring her thumbnail to her mouth, then snatched it back down again.

Come on, Lu, you can do this, Raquel thought, wishing twin telepathy were a real thing.

After a long pause, Lu tilted her head. "It doesn't look *that* bad," she said, keeping her eyes on the floor.

What was she doing? Raquel thought. "I bet Mom could cut it for you!" she almost shouted.

"*Uf!* Not *that* bad?" Dad pressed his hand over his chest as though they had wounded him. "I guess that settles it. But your mom is too busy to give me a haircut. I'll just have to cut it myself."

Raquel knew right then it had worked. Even Lu could hardly contain a smile. Dad had said the magic words.

Mom coughed as if she had swallowed a bug. "You certainly *will not* just do it yourself." She stood and dusted bits of thread off her lap. "Kel, go find a comb. I'll be right back with my shears." Then she stomped down the hall, muttering to herself, "Everyone thinks they can just cut their own hair. Like it's *so* easy. I'll tell you what's not easy: having to look at a terrible DIY haircut every day."

Raquel grabbed Lu's wrist on her way to the bathroom.

"It's working!" she whispered, her voice raising to a squeal.

"Yeah," Lu agreed. "I kind of . . . can't believe it."

Raquel pulled open one drawer and then another, looking for a comb. Finally, she found one and set it on the counter. "There's just one other thing."

"*Another* thing?" Lu asked. "Isn't this *enough*?"

"Of course not. Now we have to text Juliette," she said. "Give me your phone."

"What for?" Lu asked, but instinctively, she handed it over.

Raquel started typing. "We've got to get her to send Sylvia over. *Right now.*"

Lu tried to grab the phone back, but Raquel pulled it out of reach.

"Kel, what are you doing? If Sylvia comes over now, she'll see what's going on."

"Exactly." Raquel pressed Send and tossed the phone back.

15

Mom draped an old towel over Dad's shoulders and started to snip as Lucinda and Raquel watched from the kitchen table.

"Has Juliette replied yet?" Raquel whispered. "Is her mom coming?"

"Juliette said she'd try." She paused. "But, Raquel, I'm wondering if we should call it off. What if—"

"Just *trust* me for once."

Lucinda wanted to trust Raquel. But she couldn't stop worrying about what might happen if—*when?*—Sylvia showed up. Would she be angry and jealous? Or sad and betrayed? Lucinda wasn't sure which was worse.

But then she followed Raquel's gaze to the kitchen. Mom's face was focused but calm. Dad sat up straight, his eyes closed and his shoulders relaxed. Maybe it was worth it.

Slowly, without their parents noticing, Raquel lifted her phone and snapped a picture.

The knock on the back door window startled them all.

"Gah!" Lucinda jumped out of her chair and nearly knocked a picture frame off the wall behind her. "It's Sylvia!" She pointed at the door. Sylvia was on the other side of the door, smiling and waving.

"Calm down," Raquel said through clenched teeth.

Dad started to get up, but Mom was still holding a piece of his hair. "Wait, hang on!" she said. "I'll be right there. Let me just find a mask."

Raquel stood. "That's okay, I'll get it." She grabbed one of Mom's homemade masks off the table and put it on, then walked across the kitchen and swept open the door. "Oh, hey, Sylvia! We didn't see you there. Dad's a little busy right now. Mom is giving him a haircut."

Sylvia took a step back from the doorway. Lucinda's heart began to thump.

But if Sylvia was angry or upset—or even just slightly annoyed—she didn't show it.

"I can see that" was all she said, her smile never wavering.

"So . . . did you need something?" Raquel asked. "Otherwise, we should probably close the door so Crybaby doesn't escape." He was sniffing curiously at Sylvia's toes.

"Actually, Jules sent me over," Sylvia said. She looked past Raquel at Lucinda. "She said you had something for her. Something important?"

"Oh!" Lucinda had been so nervous she'd almost forgotten. "Right! I'll go get it." She was grateful for a reason to leave the room. At the same time, though she didn't want to miss anything. As she dashed down the hall, she strained to hear what was happening. Mom asked if Juliette was feeling any better, and Sylvia answered that she seemed tired but fine.

Lucinda returned, panting, a minute later, her resistance band looped over her shoulder.

"What's this?" Sylvia asked. She reached out for the band without stepping inside the house.

"I use it for core strength and balance mainly," Lucinda explained, stretching her arm to give it to her. "But Juliette can probably find some different exercises online. I just thought she might want to borrow it since she can't go out running right now."

Raquel glanced up from her phone with a questioning look.

What? Lucinda mouthed back. It had been the best excuse she could come up with to get Sylvia over to the house. She was proud of her quick thinking, to be honest.

"That is so kind of you," Sylvia said. "I'm sure Jules will appreciate it."

Lucinda looked at her feet. "I just know how much I hate to miss a workout."

Sylvia didn't reply. She was watching Mom now, studying her as she checked to make sure Dad's sideburns were even.

"I wonder . . . " Sylvia started to say. Lucinda couldn't tell at first whether she was talking to herself or to the rest of them.

"Andrea, I wonder if you've ever thought about making a tutorial," Sylvia said again, a little louder. "A video, I mean. To show people how to cut their own hair. Or . . . maybe their family's hair? How to do it at home, I mean, now that all the salons are closed."

Lucinda recognized the eager glint in her eye, the same look Raquel had whenever she was excited about a new idea.

Mom threw her head back and laughed. "Me? I don't think so." She whipped the towel off Dad's shoulders like a magician revealing a transformation. That had always been Lucinda's favorite part of watching Mom work. The before and after. "No one wants to see that."

"Are you kidding?" Sylvia said. "People would love it. I could produce it. Raquel might even have some footage we can use."

Raquel's phone fell with a thwack on the tabletop. They all turned toward her.

"Were you filming this, Kel?" Dad asked as he brushed bits of hair off his neck. "What for?"

Pink blotches spread over Raquel's cheeks. "Oh . . . just a . . . project for school," she sputtered.

Sylvia's face brightened. "Maybe we can work on it together! I'd love to help."

"Maybe," Raquel mumbled.

Sylvia took another step away from the doorway, starting to leave. "I better get back to Jules," she said. "Thanks again, Lucinda. And, Andrea, think about that video!"

"We'll see," Mom said. She reached into the pantry for the broom. "I'll have the girls bring over some dinner later anyway."

Dad stood in the doorway. He pressed his hand over his heart. Sylvia put a hand over hers before waving and setting out for the loft.

It was a lucky thing Raquel hadn't seen that, Lucinda thought. Although a part of her wished she had. A part of her wondered if seeing Dad so quietly happy would change Raquel's mind, or if it would only make her fight harder to drive Sylvia away.

But Raquel had already bounded to the sofa and was gesturing for Lucinda to follow her.

"Look at this," she said.

Lucinda folded her legs underneath her and pulled Crybaby onto her lap. Then she leaned over Raquel's glowing phone screen.

It showed Mom and Dad in the kitchen, both of them smiling as Mom lifted a section of his hair with the comb. At the very edge of the frame Sylvia peered in through the back door window. Raquel had managed to capture the moment just before Sylvia's knock had surprised them.

They studied it, Lucinda trying once again to find any trace of jealousy on Sylvia's face. She couldn't, though she tried to disguise her relief. "I guess she didn't really seem to mind, did she?"

"Who cares about her?" Raquel said. "Look at *them*!"

Lucinda shifted her focus. Mom and Dad seemed peaceful. They seemed at home. Lucinda suddenly wished she could climb into the photo and live in that moment a little longer.

But then Raquel took back the phone and tapped on the screen. With a swoosh, the image was delivered to the whole newspaper club.

Replies flickered on-screen.

It worked!

SO romantic!

This is better than TV!

And the last one:

#TeamAndrea

16

Raquel let Lu run ahead of her as they crossed through the orange trees toward the loft apartment. It was early evening, but the sun still glowed soft and golden. Dad had packed two plates full of chicken tostadas into a grocery bag for Sylvia and Juliette. The apartment had a kitchen. They could have made their own dinner. But Dad had insisted on cooking for them, too.

The plastic bag knocked against Raquel's hip as she walked, not really paying attention to where she was stepping. She didn't have to. She and Lu could make that walk in their sleep after all the summers they had spent at the ranchette. With her free hand, she scrolled through the messages that had pinged into the *Manzanita Mirror* group text. #TeamAndrea. It felt good to think of the four of them as a team. It felt good to think of them winning.

She reread the last message, from Daisy. *Just keep up the pressure and Sylvia will be gone for good.*

"What's taking you so long?" Lu called back to her. Raquel put the phone in her pocket and jogged to catch up.

Lu was staring up at the windows above the barn. Lights flickered inside. Someone must have had the television on.

"I guess we should . . . knock?" Lu asked.

They never had to knock before. Then again, there had never been strangers (practically) in the loft before. Lu started up the steps that led to the apartment.

"Wait!" Raquel stopped her. "Let's go the other way." An oak tree grew behind the barn, with branches that stretched up to the bedroom window. Maybe they could peek inside and get Juliette's attention without Sylvia noticing.

"You go," Raquel said when they got to the tree. "One of us has to hold the dinner bag, and you climb faster."

Lu nodded and tightened the sweatshirt she had tied around her waist. She scrambled up the branches, and when she got to the window, she whispered down to Raquel, "Juliette's in the bedroom . . . And her mom's not with her."

"Good. Get her to come to the window!"

Lu stretched out her hand to reach a bunch of acorns. She threw them, one at a time, at the window. The first one missed and bounced off the wall, but the next one hit the window with a soft thud.

"She's coming!" Lu said.

Raquel flinched as the old window screeched open. They needed to keep quiet if they were going to have a chance to talk to Juliette without her mom hearing.

"You scared me!" Juliette said, poking her head out the window. She didn't seem sick, Raquel thought, judging by how she was almost shouting. "You look sort of like a burglar with that mask on. A burglar with a taste for vintage florals, but still."

"Shh!" Raquel warned.

Juliette looked down. "You're here, too? What's going on?"

"We brought dinner," Lu said, still hugging the branch.

"And we wanted to ask you about your mom," Raquel added, trying to get to the point. "What happened when she got back from the house this afternoon? How did she seem to you?"

"Just what I texted Lu earlier," Juliette said.

Lu? And they were texting? Why hadn't Lu mentioned it? Raquel wondered.

"She seemed pretty normal," Juliette continued. "She said Marcos got a haircut . . . Oh! And she has a new idea for a cool vlog series about quarantine style tips or something."

"She mentioned the haircut?" Raquel asked. "Was she angry? *Jealous?*"

Juliette's eyebrows wrinkled. "That's not why you wanted me to send her over, is it? Mom doesn't really get jealous." She glanced over her shoulder. "Shh! I think she heard something!"

On the other side of the barn, the apartment door opened and Sylvia stepped out onto the landing.

"Hello? Is somebody out there? Marcos, amor, is that you?"

Raquel wanted to gag. Instead, she held a finger to her lips, signaling to Juliette and her sister to stay quiet.

"It's just me," she said, walking back to the stairs. "I brought you guys some dinner."

"Oh, hello, Kel," Sylvia said. "I thought I heard voices, but I wasn't sure. I'm still getting used to all the sounds out here." She took a step backward into the apartment as Raquel climbed the steps and set the dinner bag on the landing.

"Smells delicious," Sylvia said, lifting the bag. "Thank you. I love your face mask, by the way. I meant to tell you earlier. I don't think I've ever seen one like that before. All of mine are so plain."

Raquel's hand went to her face. In the beginning of all this, she didn't think she'd ever get used to the masks, but now she sometimes forgot she was wearing one.

"Mom made it," she said. "Out of some vintage fabric she found in the house. She made a bunch, actually. She's very talented."

Sylvia smiled. "What a good idea. I'll have to ask her to upcycle some of my old things, too."

Raquel started down the stairs. "You can try," she said. "But Mom is pretty busy with her own projects. And helping Dad, of course."

"Of course," Sylvia agreed. "Well, tell him we said thank you for dinner, and have a safe walk back!"

The door shut, and Raquel crept around to the back of the barn.

Lu was still in the tree, talking to Juliette.

"Then the meet got canceled, of course," Juliette was saying. "And it's just really frustrating because I was *so* close to breaking the school's long-jump record."

Lu groaned sympathetically. "I know how you feel. I'm supposed to be getting ready for this big figure skating competition, but my rink's been closed for weeks. Hey, maybe we should train together, while we're both waiting for everything to get back to normal. When you're allowed out of the house, I mean."

Lu was supposed to be plotting with Juliette, not coordinating workout schedules.

"Come on, Lu, we have to go," Raquel said. "Juliette's mom is going to call her to dinner any second, and anyway, I have a newspaper story to finish."

Lu looked down. "Oh, hey, Raquel. I didn't hear you come back." She started easing her way back down the tree. "Talk to you later, Jules!"

Jules?

Raquel felt a tug at her chest, like her sister was pulling further away. She tried to ignore it.

But as she led the way back to the apartment, she said, "You know, you probably shouldn't make friends with her. Considering we're trying to sabotage her mom's relationship and everything."

"She's not so bad," Lucinda answered. "You might even like her if you gave her a chance."

Raquel wasn't sure whom she was talking about, Sylvia or Juliette. And for once she didn't want to ask.

17

Hi! How are things going down there? Has the rink opened yet?

Hey there! Nope, still closed. Don't worry, you're not missing out. How's your family?

Pretty good. Guess what! I think I might have found a new workout partner! My dad's girlfriend's daughter.

Although she wanted to bury her head under her pillow when the alarm Raquel set trilled at six a.m. on Monday morning, Lucinda forced her eyes open. With the farm stand closed until Thursday, it was Dad's day to sleep in, and since Mom didn't need to help him, she could sleep in, too. That meant Lucinda would have time to talk to Raquel—without their parents overhearing—before they logged in for school.

Crybaby stood, stretched, and whined a complaint about the early hour. Then he curled back onto her pillow and sank into sleep again.

"Lucky," Lucinda said, yawning. She got up and did ten jumping jacks to jolt herself awake, then tiptoed down the hall in search of Raquel.

She knew exactly where she'd find her. They might have been more than three hundred miles from their apartment in Los Angeles, but it was still Monday.

"Let me guess, you're on deadline?"

Raquel lifted her eyes over the top of the laptop and swallowed a mouthful of Corn Chex. "How'd you know?"

But when Lucinda walked around the table and looked over Raquel's shoulder at the computer screen, she saw a website for a coffee shop in Stockton, a bigger city just south of Lockeford.

"What's Café Mozart?" Lucinda asked, squinting, her eyes still a little bleary.

"It's where Mom and Dad had their first date," she said. "Don't you remember? We stopped there on the way to Lockeford when we came up to visit for Christmas in second grade."

Lucinda sat down next to her, bewildered. "How do you remember, like, *every* tiny thing?" She pulled Raquel's cereal bowl toward her and took a bite.

"I just pay attention when it matters," Raquel said,

taking the cereal back. "Anyway, I was thinking about what Daisy said, about trying to re-create their first date. But the coffee place doesn't deliver. And since we can't exactly drive there, we're going to have to come up with another plan."

"Actually, that's . . . something I've been wanting to talk to you about," Lucinda said.

Raquel spun toward her, eyebrows raised eagerly. "You have another idea? What is it?"

Lucinda picked at her thumbnail. "Not exactly." She had fallen asleep thinking about what she would say to her sister. She tried to remember the words now. "It's just that, everything went so well last night, I was wondering if maybe we should just . . . let things happen on their own from now on." She loved the idea of bringing Mom and Dad closer together, but the thought of any more tricks made her stomach hurt. Plus, she meant what she said coming home from the loft. About Jules not being so bad. She liked having her around, actually. She liked having a friend.

Raquel looked at her as if she had just suggested they

make Crybaby editor in chief of the *Manzanita Mirror.*

"Do you want to know why we can't just let things happen on their own?" she asked. "I'll show you." She got up and went to the laundry room, then came back with a purple basket filled with clothes. "I found this sitting right inside the back door when I got up this morning. She even left a *note*." Raquel slammed a pink scrap of paper on the table. She watched with her arms folded while Lucinda read.

Thank you for taking care of this for me! XO Sylvia

Lucinda read it three times, and then a fourth, but she still didn't understand what Raquel was so upset about.

Raquel snatched the note back and huffed. "Do you *want* to keep finding her laundry around here? Like this is *her* place? Like she's taking over? Ordering us around?"

"Not when you put it that way," Lucinda said, shrinking backward.

"Well, *that's* why we have to get her out of here."

Lucinda twisted her fingers together, not daring to raise her eyes. "Raquel, I'm sorry, but I think you might be overreacting," she managed to murmur. But there was more. "What if we . . . tried giving Sylvia the benefit of the doubt? It was just a small favor."

Both of them stared at the laundry basket for a moment. Then Raquel pulled a leopard-print blouse off the top. "Wait a minute." She grinned. "Maybe you're right. Maybe all she wanted was a favor."

Lucinda hoped that, by the time Ms. King said they could log off at the end of the school day, Raquel would have changed her mind. (Not that she ever changed her mind once she had an idea in her head.) But when Raquel launched the newspaper meeting that afternoon and the screen began to fill with faces, the first thing she said was "I have an announcement. I've decided to postpone the story I had been planning to write about the curbside library service Mrs. Forrest is starting. Instead, Lu and I will be writing a step-by-step guide to making your own face mask. But we need your opinion."

They had taken the computer to the bedroom, where they sat on the floor with Sylvia's laundry basket between them. Raquel held up two tops, one in each hand. "Should we start with leopard, or with stripes?"

Raquel told the newspaper club what she'd already told Lucinda. How the night before, Sylvia complimented her upcycled face mask and said she wished Andrea would make her some of her own. And how that very morning, a pile of Sylvia's clothes appeared in the house.

"At first, I thought she wanted *us* to do her laundry," Raquel explained. "But that doesn't make any sense. She's obviously capable of doing her own chores. As Lu *so helpfully* pointed out, Sylvia was asking for a favor: She obviously wants us to turn these clothes into face masks."

"*Or* she wanted Dad to wash them," Lucinda said for the tenth time. But she could see Raquel was determined, and that the nodding faces on the computer screen would only encourage her.

Lucinda covered her face with her hands. "Please, Kel, this is *such* a terrible idea. We should at least double-check to make sure this is what Sylvia actually wanted. Let me text Jules first."

"What's so terrible about it?" Peter asked. One of the cockatiels warbled in the background. "Recycling clothes is good for the environment."

"Yeah," Mira Young said. "I think it sounds fun. It would give people something to do, anyway."

"We're going to get in *so* much trouble," Lucinda pleaded. Sylvia would be angry. Mom and Dad would be furious. And Jules? Lucinda imagined how she would feel if someone cut up Mom's clothes. She shuddered.

"Not necessarily," Raquel insisted. "Maybe she'll *thank* us. Anyway, she should have been clearer about what she was asking for."

Alice unmuted herself. "I agree with Kel. I think you should go for it. Team Andrea!"

The chat box filled with messages.

Do it!

I vote for face masks!

Plus, you could donate some!

#TeamAndrea

#TeamAndrea

#TeamAndrea

Lucinda squeezed her eyes shut as Raquel held the scissors against the leopard-print blouse. "I can't watch."

She heard the blades slice through the fabric, heard the cheers that erupted from the screen. She opened her eyes again just in time to see Raquel lift the blouse up the camera to show the rectangle-shaped hole in the back.

Raquel offered her the scissors. "Try it. It's so satisfying."

"Come on, Lucinda, go for it!" Alice urged.

"Yeah, Lucinda!" Mira said. "Do the stripes."

Lucinda shook her head and turned away.

"Cut! Cut! Cut!" the faces on the screen chanted.

"*Fine!* Just stop, okay?!"

Lucinda almost never yelled. The computer went silent. She turned to Raquel. "You too. If I do this, can we just *stop*?"

Raquel nodded. So Lucinda picked up the scissors.

Her sister had been right. Something about the way the fabric gave a soft *crunch* as the scissors cut through felt like tearing into all the disappointment and confusion and uncertainty of the past two months. When she finished, the whole club cheered. Lucinda could almost forget these were Sylvia's clothes, and she felt herself reach back into the laundry basket for another shirt.

Just as Dad pushed the door open. He was on a video call, holding the phone in front of his face.

Lucinda dropped the scissors, and Raquel spun the laptop around so it faced the wall.

"You two haven't seen Sylvia's laundry, have you? She dropped it off this morning, but I can't find—" Dad looked down and saw the overturned basket, the pile of fabric scraps, the scissors. "Oh no."

"What happened? What's going on?" The sound of Sylvia's worried voice made Lucinda almost dizzy with embarrassment over what they'd done.

Dad turned the phone around. "Sylvia, I am so sorry."

Lucinda's cheeks burned as she saw Sylvia squint into the screen and gasp. "Is that my . . . ? I was going to wear that to a videoconference with a client this afternoon. It's my lucky shirt. What happened?"

"I don't know what could have gotten into them." Then he narrowed his eyes at Lucinda and Raquel. "But I'm going to find out."

Hearing the commotion, Mom rushed in. "What's going on in here?

"I *told* you!" Lucinda cried.

"Told her what?" Mom demanded.

Lucinda wanted to answer, but Raquel put a hand on top of hers. *Leave this to me*, she told her wordlessly.

"Nothing's going on. We're making some face masks. Just like Sylvia asked us to."

18

"Like I *asked* you to?" Sylvia's voice rose. "I never asked—"

"Of course you did," Raquel went on. "When I saw you last night. Don't you remember? You were saying how much you loved the face masks Mom made us and how you wondered if she'd make you some, too. So when I saw your clothes just *dumped* here this morning, I thought that's what you wanted. And since Mom is so busy, me and Lu decided to be helpful and get a head start on the cutting. What's everyone so upset about? Did you change your mind?"

No one said anything for a few long seconds. Then Dad shook his head. "Raquel, this is ridiculous. You can't expect us to believe that you really thought Sylvia wanted you to *destroy* her clothing. Tell me the truth. What's going on here?"

Lu stared at the carpet, chewing on one of her fingernails. *Typical*, Raquel thought. She glanced at Mom, who stood behind Dad, arms crossed and looking even angrier than he did. Raquel glanced away. Clearly neither of them was going to be any help. As usual, she'd have to handle this on her own.

She opened her mouth to answer when Sylvia cut in.

"Marcos, no. She's telling the truth. That's exactly what happened. This was all a . . . a misunderstanding."

Raquel was stunned. She didn't know if Sylvia actually believed her, or if she was just afraid to hear the truth that Dad had asked for. Either way, Raquel wasn't going to interrupt.

Mom took the phone from Dad's hands and held it up to her face. "Sylvia, you don't have to do this. They need to be held responsible."

Sylvia forced a laugh that sounded more like the choking cough of someone who had taken a bite of something that was spicier than she expected. "No, it's *my* fault. I should have . . . left a note. It's actually kind of funny when you think about it, you know? And the girls did me a favor, really. Now I'll have some new face masks *and* the perfect excuse to do some online shopping."

"See?" Raquel said, gazing up at her parents. "It was all a misunderstanding."

Mom wasn't convinced, though. A day later, she still hadn't let it go, even after Sylvia had said they should all forget it ever happened.

"I cannot believe you would do something like that, Raquel," Mom said on Tuesday afternoon. "Or that you would go along with it, Lucinda. I'm so disappointed in both of you." They were in the vegetable garden, pulling up weeds and thinning out the carrots. Mom insisted they pay Sylvia back for the ruined clothing and put them to work right after school to start earning the money they owed.

"We said we were sorry," Raquel replied. "Anyway,

none of this would have happened if Sylvia had just done her *own* laundry, right, Lu?"

Lu inched over to the cauliflowers a few rows over, her earbuds firmly in place. Raquel should've known she wouldn't back her up.

Well, so what if they had to spend the rest of the quarantine pulling weeds? It would be worth it. They had finally flustered Sylvia. Everyone on the newspaper staff agreed. They had heard the whole thing.

Raquel's phone buzzed. She looked up to make sure Mom wasn't watching and pulled it from her pocket.

Daisy

> I can't stop thinking about it. I wish I could have seen her face! #TeamAndrea

Raquel

> She was pretty surprised, that's for sure.

"That better not be a phone I see, Raquel," Mom warned.

Raquel

> Sorry. Can't text right now.

OK. We can catch up later. Just promise to tell me everything that happens next.

Raquel put the phone back in her pocket. She wasn't exactly sure what would happen next. She just wished Lu was as determined as she was to be part of it.

She looked over at her sister, spraying the cauliflower with a hose. Lu closed her eyes and took small, criss-cross steps over the soil before swinging her right leg out behind her and holding it in the air. She was practicing her ice skating routine, Raquel knew. If she worked that hard on bringing their family back together, Sylvia would be gone by now. Or almost, anyway.

But since the face mask incident, Lu had been unusually quiet, even for her. She opened her eyes and looked over the cauliflower.

"You know what this reminds me of?" Lu asked.

Finally! Actual words.

"What?"

"Those pickles we made with Tía Maggie. Look, all the ingredients are right here."

Raquel gazed around the vegetable garden. "Carrots, cauliflower, onion."

Mom had been kneeling in the dirt, thinning a row of carrots. She sat up and retied the bandanna she wore to keep her hair off her face. "It's called escabeche," she said. "And you're right. It looks like we're only missing the jalapeños."

Tía Maggie was Dad's aunt. She lived with her daughter, Cousin Sara, now, but a few years ago, Mom had begged her to teach them how to make the vinegary escabeche she always served alongside tortas and tostadas.

"Remember how upset Tía Maggie got when Mom cut the carrots too small?" Lu said. "How she took the knife away and made her peel instead."

Mom laughed. "Tía Maggie is . . . meticulous," she said. "But for good reason. If the carrots are too small, they get mushy." She paused. "I miss her sometimes. It's nice, every now and then, to have someone to tell you the right way to do things."

"That's interesting," Raquel muttered. "You never

seem to think it's nice when *I* tell you the right way."

This time Lu laughed. "That's because you only *think* you know the right way." Then she turned the hose toward her and sprayed.

"Hey!" Raquel yelled, springing up to dodge the water. But it was a relief to hear Mom and Lu laugh again. To know they wouldn't stay angry forever. That she was back on their team.

Lu turned off the water. "What if we go visit Tía Maggie?" she said. "We could bring her some escabeche."

Raquel's first thought was *No!* They needed to get Mom and Dad to spend time together while they still had the chance, not send Mom out of the house for what could end up being hours. But then she realized Lu might be onto something. They couldn't re-create Mom and Dad's first date, but maybe they could help Mom remember what it was like to be part of Dad's family again. And the best part was, it had all been *Lu's* idea.

"Can we?" Raquel said.

Mom shook her head. "I don't think so. I'm sorry, amor-citas. I would love to see her," she said. "But it's not a good time to visit right now. We want to keep Tía Maggie healthy."

Of course. Even though it had been months since they first heard about the mysterious new sickness that was keeping everyone at home, even though it was all anyone seemed to talk about sometimes, Raquel still managed to forget that nothing was normal right now, that they couldn't just get in the car and visit their tía. Still, she wasn't ready to give up.

"Maybe we can wave through the window, at least," she said.

"And drop off the escabeche on the doorstep," Lu added.

Mom looked from one to the other and sighed. "I'm no match for the two of you," she said. "All right, we'll see what your dad thinks. For now, Lu, you pick out a nice cauliflower and Kel, dig up some carrots and onions. I'll see if I can find some peppers."

Once Mom's back was turned, Raquel took her phone out of her pocket snapped a photo. She wanted to remember all the ingredients—cauliflower and carrots, dirt and laughter—that would bring them back together again.

19

It wasn't cold outside anymore, but going to the ice rink after school twice a week had gotten Lucinda in the habit of tying a sweatshirt around her waist wherever she went. You never knew when you might need it. This time, she whipped it off, and she and Mom and Raquel filled it with carrots, onions, and cauliflower that they bundled up and carried back to the house. Their shoes were caked with mud, and dirt clung to the undersides of their fingernails by the time they got back, but Lucinda didn't mind. It was the most fun she'd had since they had gotten to Lockeford over the weekend.

They stomped their feet on the back doormat before walking inside, where Crybaby was waiting to greet them with a sad whine.

"Did you think we abandoned you?" Lucinda said. "Don't worry, we're home."

He meowed and sniffed at Mom's feet, then peeked outside the door as if hoping to see where they had been.

"Get inside," Mom said, nudging him gently back with her toe. "You don't want to get lost out there."

Lucinda brought the vegetables into the kitchen, where Dad was eating spoonfuls of leftover rice over the sink. She lifted the sweatshirt onto the counter, and an onion rolled out, nearly tumbling onto the floor.

Dad leaped forward and caught it. "What's all this?" he asked.

"We're making escabeche," Lucinda said brightly.

"To take to Tía Maggie tomorrow," Raquel added. "Mom really misses her. You know how close they are."

"I do miss her, but, like I told you outside, we're only going *if* your dad agrees it's a good idea," Mom said, following them into the kitchen. She turned to Dad. "What do you think? We can leave the escabeche on Sara's porch and maybe say hello through the window?"

Dad folded his arms over his chest. "Hmm," he said, his forehead wrinkled as if he needed to give it careful thought. But Lucinda could already see the beginnings of a smile flicker at the corners of his eyes.

"I think..." he said, pausing dramatically. "We're going to need some mason jars. And I'm pretty sure I saw some in the basement."

After they all washed their hands, Mom cleared off the countertop while Lucinda and Raquel scrubbed the soil off the vegetables. Dad went to the pantry to find the rest of the ingredients: salt and pepper and vinegar—and picked some oregano from the mini herb garden on the windowsill.

Mom insisted on chopping the carrots herself. "As all of you know, I had a very strict teacher, and now I am an *expert* at chopping carrots," she said, tilting her chin toward the ceiling. And they all teased Dad when the onion made his eyes tear up.

As she ground up oregano leaves in Abuelita's

molcajete, Lucinda noticed Raquel take out her phone and start recording. She panned around the kitchen, probably capturing another #TeamAndrea moment that she would send off to the newspaper club.

Lucinda wished her sister would stop like she'd promised. They were supposed to be trying to bring their parents closer together, and she couldn't help but worry that all these plans—which somehow never worked out quite the way they'd hoped—would only make things worse. That if Mom ever found out about #TeamAndrea, she'd be even angrier and more embarrassed than she had been about the face masks.

Lucinda had been thinking a lot about what Coach J'Marie told her the last time she sent a panicked text, wondering if the rinks would open in time for her to prepare for the Pacific Coast Classic.

Coach J'Marie

> You can't control when the rinks will reopen. And you definitely won't make them open any faster worrying about it. All you can control is what you do with this situation. Keep yourself healthy. Keep yourself strong.

No matter how stubborn Raquel was, they couldn't control whether Dad came back or Sylvia went away. Maybe they could keep their family healthy and strong, though. And scheming seemed like a bad way to do it.

For now, at least, Raquel was distracted at the stove helping Dad sauté the vegetables in olive oil. Mom ordered pizzas for dinner—one for the house and one for the loft—since there were a lot of jars to fill and the kitchen was going to be too busy to cook in.

The drive to Cousin Sara's house the next day was a short one, especially since there still weren't many cars on the road. Mom let them take the afternoon off school, so they left at lunchtime, right after Dad had finished his morning chores in the orange grove.

"It's weird how empty everything is," Raquel murmured as they looked out the back-seat windows of Dad's truck.

"Like everyone's on vacation or something," Lucinda agreed. It had been quieter back home in Los Angeles, too, but there were still buses running and customers waiting their turn to grocery shop, standing with their carts spaced six feet apart in lines that stretched all the way around the parking lot.

They hardly saw anyone on the way to visit Tía Maggie. They drove past dark restaurants with "Closed" signs in the windows and a park where someone had taken down the basketball hoops and blocked off the playground with yellow caution tape. When Dad stopped on Cousin Sara's street, with nobody out riding bikes or washing their cars in the driveway, Lucinda got the eerie feeling that they might be the only people left on the planet.

But that only lasted until they got to Cousin Sara's porch.

The whole family was waiting on the other side of the big picture window: Cousin Sara and Cousin Sergio and their three kids, all teenagers. Tía Maggie, in her wheel-chair, was positioned in the middle, and she waved at them with both hands. In a second, the world felt full again.

"Ay!" Mom cried as she galloped up the stairs as if she might reach in and hug Tía Maggie right through the window. Instead, Mom held her hand against the glass. "¿Cómo ha estado?"

Tía Maggie's voice sounded muffled and far away, but they could still hear her. "Pues, I've been doing fine, mija. You look like you're doing well, too."

"¡Sí!" Mom nodded. "We're all doing so well."

Raquel held up the basket of escabeche jars. "Look what we brought!"

"Mmm, our favorite," Cousin Sara said.

Tía Maggie raised one eyebrow. "Pero, you didn't chop the zanahorias too small, did you?"

Dad leaned toward the window and said, "No se preocupe, Tía, I was supervising."

Mom socked him playfully in the shoulder, and Tía Maggie said, "Pues, now I *am* worried."

It was like landing the perfect double toe loop. Better than Lucinda could have ever imagined. She held her phone up to the glass to show them a video of her latest skating program, and Dad promised to come back with cherries as soon as they were ripe.

Raquel wanted a selfie before they left, and all ten of them managed to squeeze into the frame, even though they had to stay on opposite sides of the window. "On the count of three, say, 'Quarantine!'"

Raquel looked down at the camera. "Got it," she said.

Then, as they started back toward the truck, Lucinda saw Dad put his arm around Mom's shoulder.

Lucinda froze. She sucked in a breath of air, startled but also satisfied. She grabbed Raquel's hand. "Look!" she whispered.

Raquel lifted her phone to take a picture, but Lucinda stopped her.

"No, don't," she said. It wasn't a #TeamAndrea moment. It was a #TeamMendoza moment, and the only people who needed to see it already had.

And before she could really savor it, the moment was over. Dad's cell phone buzzed. He pulled his arm away from Mom to answer it.

"Hey!"

Lucinda and Raquel exchanged a glance.

"Yeah, we're heading back right now," Dad said before a long pause. They watched his face carefully. Then he said, "Really? Oh, that is *great* news."

20

It was *not* great news. It was pretty much the worst news, actually. Sylvia called to say that since Juliette hadn't shown any more symptoms, and since she never had a fever, her doctor felt it was safe for her to come out of isolation.

All right, that part, the part where Juliette wasn't sick, that *was* good news. But the rest of it was not. Sylvia and Juliette were going to spend one more night in the loft apartment to finish the television series they'd been binge-watching together. But after that, they'd be ready to move back into the house.

"As long as that's all right with Andrea," Sylvia said, her chirpy voice in the cell phone loud enough for all of them to hear as they leaned against Dad's truck and waited for the call to finish.

"It's just fine with me, Sylvia," Mom had replied. "I'm so glad to hear that Juliette is in the clear. What a relief."

But it hadn't been a relief. It had been the opposite of a relief. There were only three more days until Mom was supposed to go back to Los Angeles—three more days to get their parents back together again, which, despite what she told Lu, was what Raquel had wanted all along.

"Wait, tomorrow?" she said, standing on tiptoe to speak into Dad's phone. He switched it to the other ear. "But that's not enough time. Mom won't be able to pack. I thought we could make another batch of escabeche."

Sylvia didn't hear her. Or maybe she just didn't care. "We'll have dinner to celebrate," she said. "A big family dinner."

They had to stop this. "Me and Lu are going to wait inside the truck." Raquel opened the door and shoved Lu inside.

"Hey, what was that for?" Lu asked, rubbing her shoulder.

"Were you not listening? Sylvia is coming back!" Raquel reached into her pocket. "I'll text the club and call an emergency meeting. They'll help us figure out what to do. You text Juliette. See if *she* has any ideas. What are you waiting for? *Hurry!*"

"No," Lu said. She turned away, leaning her forehead against the window.

If she hadn't been sitting, Raquel was certain her knees would have buckled under her. "What do you mean 'no'? Mom is leaving soon. We don't have much time. We were finally making some progress. We can't ease up now."

Lu faced her again. Her eyes were determined. The only other time Raquel had ever seen her sister look like that was just before a skating competition. Did that mean they were rivals now?

"I mean no more emergency meetings, no more plotting with Jules. I mean it's time to stop. Just like you promised you would." Lu pointed out the window. "Mom and Dad are closer than ever. All of us are together. This is exactly what we wanted, Raquel. If you don't stop, if you keep pushing and pushing like you always do, you are going to ruin this. You are going to ruin everything."

Now Raquel was sitting cross-legged on the living room sofa, watching Mom, Dad, and Lu work on the puzzle that was still spread out, unfinished, over the coffee table. "You sure you don't want to join us, mija?" Dad asked. He turned a pale turquoise piece upside down and tried to fit it into corner. "We'll make room for you."

Lu scooted over. "Come on, help us," she said, as if nothing had happened back in the truck.

"No thanks." Raquel looked down at her phone again. She would have held the newspaper meeting anyway, without Lucinda. But she didn't want to miss anything that might happen between Mom and Dad on what might be their last night together.

So she did the next best thing:

Raquel

BREAKING NEWS ALERT: Sylvia wants to move back in TOMORROW.

Raquel

> We can't let this happen. Send your best ideas ASAP!!! #TeamAndrea

She waited for a response, staring at the screen so long her vision started to blur. Finally, her cell phone pinged. So did Lu's.

Daisy

> I think you should sneak into the apartment and fill her shampoo bottle with some of your mom's hair dye! There's no way she sticks around if you ruin her clothes *and* her hair.

Raquel thought about this. It wasn't a bad idea. But she wouldn't be able to pull it off on her own, and, unfortunately, she couldn't count on Lu anymore.

Alice

> What if you pretend to be sick? Everyone would have to stay separated. Plus, taking care of you will force your parents to work together. I could give you acting lessons!

Lu turned around and scowled at Raquel, then typed something into her phone.

Lucinda

Seriously? Hair dye? Acting lessons? Tell them to stop, Kel. Even you know this is over the line.

Lu hadn't sent it to the whole group. Just Raquel, and as soon as the message pinged through, she rolled her eyes and silenced her ringer.

So, fine. Maybe Lu had a point. As much as she wanted to get her parents together again, Raquel knew she could never scare them like that. She remembered the look on Sylvia's face—on all their faces—when they thought Juliette was infected. And anyway, they'd be right back where they started when Mom and Dad realized she was perfectly healthy.

"What's going on? You seem to be very popular tonight," Mom asked. She was holding a red puzzle piece that could have been the edge of a kite, or maybe a beach umbrella.

"Just newspaper stuff," Raquel said. "You know, stories, deadlines." She got up to get a glass of water from the kitchen—and to avoid any more questions.

Dad's cell phone was on the counter near the sink. It buzzed as Raquel filled her glass, and a text message notification flashed on the screen. It was from Sylvia.

Raquel glanced toward the living room. No one was watching her. They were all focused on the puzzle. Quickly, she tapped in the code she had seen Dad use to unlock the screen.

Sylvia

I'm planning chicken and apricot tajine for tomorrow. Jules and I are going to run back to the house for supplies. See you at 4. Can't wait to be home again! XO

Home? Raquel checked once more to make sure Dad wasn't looking. Then she erased the message.

"Hey, Dad, I have an idea," she said, walking back to the living room with her glass of water. "How about carnitas for dinner tomorrow?"

Sylvia and Juliette came walking across the orchard at exactly four o'clock the next afternoon. The carnitas had been simmering on the stove all day and the smell of it drifted onto the patio, where Mom was setting a tortilla warmer on the picnic table and Lu and Raquel were silently laying out forks and knives. Dad strode through the front door carrying the pot of meat.

"Perfect timing!" he said to Sylvia and Juliette. "Jules, we're all so glad to see you up and about."

Not all of us, Raquel thought.

Sylvia frowned as she looked around the patio. "What's all this?" She was carrying a cardboard box with two grocery bags and a clay pot with a dome-shaped cover inside.

Dad looked confused. "Oh," he said, placing his pot on the table, "it was such a nice afternoon, we thought we'd have dinner outside. Is that all right?"

"I mean what is all this *food*?" Sylvia said. "I had every-thing planned. I told you I was making chicken and apricot tajine." She held out the box. "Didn't you get my message?"

Mom tried to steer Lu and Raquel to the other side of the patio where they wouldn't be eavesdropping. But Raquel wriggled out from under her arm. She wanted to see *everything*.

Juliette was left standing in the middle. She looked down at her shoes and lifted the bag she was carrying higher on her shoulder.

Dad took out his phone and scrolled. "I'm sorry, I don't see any messages about dinner."

Raquel felt Lu's eyes on her, but she ignored them.

"Why don't you make the chicken," Dad went on, "and we'll eat the carnitas for lunch tomorrow? They're even better the next day."

Sylvia sighed. "No, you've gone to so much trouble," she said. "But please tell me you haven't already made dessert."

"We have not made dessert," Dad said, smiling.

Sylvia's face brightened. "Perfect, because I brought a citrus olive oil cake—we picked the oranges this morning. I'll go set everything inside for now. Jules has a surprise, too, but no peeking till I get back!"

Everyone seemed to exhale as Sylvia carried her cooking supplies to the kitchen. It hadn't been an argument exactly, Raquel admitted. But the mood had changed. #TeamSylvia wasn't going to win without a fight.

As soon as Sylvia returned to the patio, Raquel slipped inside the house. She wasn't sure what she was looking for exactly, but when she saw Sylvia's cake on the kitchen counter, she knew.

It sat on top of a crystal cake stand, golden yellow and covered in powdered sugar.

Raquel hurried to the pantry and found Dad's container of garlic powder. Then, pulse racing, she sprinkled it all over the cake. "Buen provecho," she whispered as she snapped a picture and sent it off to the newspaper club with the caption #TeamAndrea.

21

Lucinda pushed the cake around her plate, afraid to look Sylvia in the eye but unable to take another bite. Mom strategically covered her slice with a napkin, and Raquel was tossing bits of hers to the sparrows that had gathered at the edge of the cement, waiting patiently for crumbs.

Dad lifted a big forkful to his mouth and ate it. "Mmmm."

Sylvia tossed her napkin to the table. "Stop," she said. "I know you're just being polite. You don't have to eat it. None of you do."

Jules brought her plate to her nose and sniffed. "What *happened* to it? It tasted fine when I tested the batter!"

"I don't know!" Sylvia said, covering her eyes with her hands and making a noise that was like something between laughing and sobbing. "I swear, I've made this cake a thousand times, and it has *never* turned out like this before."

The cake had looked beautiful on the fancy stand Sylvia brought over from her house. But it tasted like the time Mom left a loaf of frozen garlic bread in the oven too long. Lucinda had a feeling her sister had something to do with this. She leaned closer to Raquel, who sat next to her at the picnic table.

"What did you do?" she whispered.

"*Me?*" Raquel whispered back, phony shock sprinkled all over her face like powdered sugar and whatever else she had poured on the cake. "Sylvia's the one who made it."

Lucinda kicked her under the table. Raquel needed to stop these travesuras—as Abuelita would have called them—before they got in trouble. Or before someone's feelings got hurt.

Sylvia put her fork down. "I think it's safe to say that dessert is officially over." She turned to Jules. "What do you think? Is it time for presents?"

Jules smiled. "Definitely!" She stood and got the gym bag she had brought over earlier that afternoon.

Raquel cringed. Lucinda did, too, but she suspected it was for a different reason than her sister. The thought of Sylvia buying gifts for them made her feel even worse about the whole face mask fiasco. Jules hadn't mentioned it so far. Lucinda wondered if she even knew, and if she did know, what she thought.

"Presents?" Mom said. "Sylvia, you really didn't need to."

"Oh, it's nothing," Sylvia said. "You'll see."

Jules opened the bag and pulled out two big boxes, wrapped in glittery red holiday paper.

"Sorry about the wrapping," Sylvia said. "It's all we had at the house."

"It's pretty," Lucinda said. "It reminds me of one of my skating dresses."

Raquel snorted.

"What? It *does*!" She peeled back the paper to reveal a worn box, its edges crushed, with a picture of Rollerblades on the front. Lucinda lifted the top off the box. The skates inside were a little scuffed, but hardly used.

"They were mine," Sylvia explained. "But I haven't used them in ages. I thought you might enjoy them, at least until you can skate on ice again."

"Thank you!" Lucinda said, already loosening the laces. "Can I try them out?"

Raquel glared at her and hurled a chunk of orange cake at the sparrows, who didn't seem to mind the garlic.

She hadn't even unwrapped her box yet.

"Of course!" Sylvia said. "Jules brought her skates over from the house. And we ordered a pair for you, too, Kel. They just arrived this morning. That was the *real* reason we needed another day at the loft."

"Thanks," Raquel mumbled. "But I don't skate."

Lucinda already had one skate on and was lacing up the other. She paused and turned to her sister. "Come on,

Kel, just give it a chance," she said. "Maybe you'll change your mind."

She meant about the skates, of course. But not just about the skates.

Raquel ran her finger along an edge of the wrapping paper as if she might just open it after all. Then she stopped.

"Not now."

It wasn't exactly like figure skating, Lucinda decided once she made a couple of laps around the cement. Dad and Sylvia had moved the grill and some flowerpots to the edges of the patio to give her and Jules more room.

For one thing, she had to push harder on the Rollerblades to pick up any speed, and she was pretty sure she wouldn't be able to spin in them. But after so many weeks, it was good to feel herself glide again.

"Are you sure you don't want to try, Raquel?" Dad asked. "It looks like fun. And everyone needs a quarantine hobby."

Lucinda sped toward her sister, then swooped to a stop

in front of her. "We would help you, Jules and I." She wanted to show Raquel that plans could change. That you could feel wobbly—you could even fall—and still keep going, even if it was in a new direction.

Raquel crossed her arms. "I *said*, no thanks." She looked at Lucinda like she didn't quite recognize her.

"Maybe later, then." She skated away. "Hey, I wonder if I can land a loop jump in these."

"No!" Dad, Mom, and Sylvia said all at once. Then they all started laughing.

After their laughter faded, Lucinda noticed Mom clear her plate and walk back inside the house.

When she came out again, she was carrying her duffel bag. She walked over to Raquel, squeezed both her shoulders, and whispered in her ear. Raquel turned her head away as if she didn't want to hear it. Then Mom waved to all of them. "Thank you all for a wonderful dinner— *and dessert*," she said. "I'm going to go settle into the loft."

Just like that? Had Mom been hurt that Lucinda was so excited about Sylvia's skates? Suddenly, she didn't want to be wearing them anymore. She stopped and forced herself not to chew her thumbnail. "Mom?"

"Keep skating, mija," she said. "Really. I'll come see you all in the morning."

Lucinda wanted to follow Mom to the loft, but Sylvia distracted her. "Your dad says you skate in competitions?" she asked. "I'd love to see one."

Lucinda took a last look at Mom walking through the orange trees in the twilight. Then she answered Sylvia. "I have a competition coming up in June," she said. "The Pacific Coast Classic. It's in LA, but that's not too far, really. I just hope the rinks open in time for me to get some practice in." She pushed off to the center of the patio and lifted her right leg, attempting a spiral.

"I don't think you have to worry," Sylvia said. "They'll probably cancel anyway, and you'll have plenty of time to prepare before they reschedule."

Lucinda felt her leg teeter, and she caught herself just before tumbling over. "What do you mean?" In the back of her mind, she had always known it was true, that the competition would be canceled. But she didn't want to believe it. To hear Sylvia just . . . *say it* like that—as if it was final—felt like the ground was sliding out from under her.

Sylvia leaned on Dad's shoulder. "It's so unfair, isn't it? This disease has brought so many hardships and disappointments," she said. "If there's any silver lining, it's that it also brought us all together. *Here.* I never want to leave this place."

This time it was Jules who stumbled forward, nearly crashing on the cement. Raquel jumped out of her chair and stormed inside. Lucinda's eyes widened. *Never?* She couldn't pull the skates off fast enough.

22

Raquel flipped on the lights in the dining room. The laptop was on the table, right where they had left it at the end of the school day, when it was time to get set for dinner. She sat and powered it on.

Before Mom left for the loft apartment—*abandoned* them there with Sylvia—she leaned down and whispered in Raquel's ear, "I know it doesn't seem like it right now, but I promise you, all the things that matter are still the same."

Raquel shook her head again in disgust. How could

Mom have said that? How could she *believe* it? When absolutely everything they cared about was so different. They couldn't go to school. They couldn't see their friends. They couldn't leave the house without worrying about an invisible danger floating in the air all around them. And now, when it was most important for them to come together, to take care of one another, Sylvia was forcing them apart. No one—not even her own twin—was doing anything to stop it.

Well, she wasn't going to give up. She clicked on the computer folder where she had saved the video she made of the four of them making escabeche the other night. She paused on a frame that showed Mom chopping carrots on Abuelita's cutting board, which was stained with years of salsa spills and water rings that Sylvia would never ever know the stories behind because she hadn't been there. Mom had. In the picture on her screen, Dad was reaching around Mom for a dish towel to wipe up the vinegar that had splashed out of the saucepan when Lu dumped the onions in from too high. In that frozen moment, Mom and Dad were looking right at each other, eyes glittering with surprised laughter. She could show it to anyone and they would see that Mom belonged in that kitchen just as much as the ancient cutting board that was older than any of them. And Dad belonged with her. They all belonged with one another. *To* one another.

The back door creaked open. "Everything all right in here?"

It was just like Sylvia to barge in where she wasn't wanted.

"Everything's fine," Raquel said. She expected Sylvia would go away after that, but she didn't. Instead, she walked over and sat down across from her.

"You left in such a hurry that I was a little worried." Her voice was different. Still, instead of carbonated the way it was when Dad was around.

Tears welled in Raquel's eyes all of a sudden, and she blinked hard to stop them from spilling over. She was so angry with herself for crying that it made her tear up even more. Sylvia didn't mention it, though. She didn't try to give her a hug or offer to get a Kleenex, which, in a weird way, made Raquel like her just a tiny bit.

But it didn't mean Sylvia knew anything about them.

"You shouldn't have said that to Lu, about the competition being canceled," Raquel finally managed to say without choking. "She wasn't ready. You have to give Lucinda time."

Sylvia nodded. "Thank you for telling me. I'll do my best not to make that mistake again." She pointed at the laptop. "Are you working on another project? May I see?"

Raquel's hand flew to the keyboard to close the video window. But then she stopped. She dropped her hand. Maybe she *should* show Sylvia the video. Maybe then she'd see what was so clear to Raquel.

"Go ahead," she said, and turned the laptop around.

Sylvia leaned forward. A curl fell in her face, and she tucked it behind her ear as she pressed Play.

Raquel heard Dad's voice: "Right behind you."

Then Mom's: "Careful! I'm holding a knife."

And Lu's at the stove: "It's boiling, you guys. Is it supposed to boil?"

Then Dad looks over Mom's shoulder and says, "Are you sure you aren't cutting those too small? No las haga mushy." And both of them laugh.

Raquel studied Sylvia's face as carefully as Sylvia studied the screen, looking for hints of what she might be thinking. But she couldn't find any. Sylvia paused the clip and looked back at her.

"This is a great sequence, Raquel," she said. "How you move from a wide, establishing shot of the kitchen to a tighter shot of your mom and dad at the counter. But look here." Sylvia moved to the chair next to Raquel and positioned the laptop between them.

It wasn't that she necessarily *wanted* to be getting video advice from Sylvia at that moment. In fact, if someone had asked her ten minutes earlier, Raquel probably would have said it was the last thing in the whole world she wanted. But Sylvia was so eager and interested that Raquel couldn't resist hearing more.

"I think," Sylvia said, making small adjustments with the keyboard, "you have just a little too much headroom above your dad. But if you were to crop it a bit ... There! Better, right?"

The frame seemed to draw Raquel in now. She wasn't just looking at it. She was almost a part of it. "Thanks."

"Anytime," Sylvia said. "I mean it. You have excellent instincts and a strong perspective. That makes all the difference."

She pushed the laptop back toward Raquel and stood. "I hope I get to see more of your videos—and I hope we see you outside again."

So that's what this was all about. Sylvia wasn't really trying to help her. She probably wasn't even really interested in her video. She was just trying to save her "big family dinner."

Well, that was too bad. Because Raquel was trying to save something more important: her family.

At last, Sylvia left. The back door swung gently behind her, but it didn't close all the way. Raquel got up to shut it, but with her hand hovering just over the doorknob, she changed her mind. Sylvia should have thought of that herself. Crybaby was safe inside the bedroom for the night, but what would Dad and Lu think, Raquel wondered, if they saw that Sylvia was so careless about something so important?

23

Lucinda paused halfway up the staircase that led to the loft apartment. Maybe she should have gone to check on Raquel. But that's probably what her sister was expecting. That Lucinda would follow her the way she always did. Raquel probably had an emergency newspaper club meeting all set up and everything. She was probably telling everyone all about what happened at dinner, and they were probably figuring out new ideas for how to chase Sylvia off once and for all. #TeamAndrea.

The thing was, she was on Team Andrea, too. Which

was why she wanted to be with Mom right now. She climbed the rest of the stairs and turned the doorknob. It was unlocked.

"Mom?" Lucinda said as she pushed open the door.

"In here!"

The whole loft probably could have fit on Dad's patio. To the right as you walked through the door, there was a bedroom that was barely big enough to hold a full-size bed and a short brown dresser. On the other side of the entryway was a sort of living room with a foldout couch where they used to build tent forts with their cousins when they all visited during the summer. Straight back was the bathroom and the kitchen with a refrigerator, a sink, a two-burner stove, and a small, square table. Dad and Abuelito had built it themselves using some of the wood from an oak tree that fell over in a windstorm. Mom once said it was her favorite piece of furniture ever.

See, Lucinda could remember important details, too.

Mom sat at the table with Abuelita's old sewing machine. It made a *chuk chuk chuk chuk* sound as her foot pressed down on the pedal. Even though the loft was so much smaller than the house, and even though the sewing machine was so old and clunky, Mom seemed at home here, Lucinda thought. Maybe more at home than she had been all week. Lucinda pulled out the chair across from her and sat down.

Mom took her foot off the sewing machine pedal. "Did you have fun skating?" she asked. She snipped a piece of thread, then placed a finished face mask on a pile with some others.

"It wasn't *that* fun," Lucinda said, taking a spool of thread out of Mom's sewing box. "It was just okay."

"Hmm," Mom said. "It looked fun. And it was pretty generous of Sylvia to give you the skates." She took two pieces of fabric—more of the rectangles they had cut earlier that week, Lucinda realized—matched the corners, and started to pin them together.

"Really?" Lucinda asked. "You didn't feel..." She looked down at her lap. "I don't know. Left out...or anything?"

Mom put down the fabric and stuck the pin she was holding back in the pincushion. "No," she said. "Not left out. I won't lie, this week hasn't exactly been easy for me—but then, it hasn't been easy for anyone, has it? We're all doing our best, aren't we? Sylvia seems like a good person. She cares about what you care about. How could I have a problem with that?"

Lu rolled the spool back and forth on the table. "Then, how come you left?"

Mom took the spool away and gave Lucinda a roll of elastic and some scissors. "Here, if you need something to keep your hands busy, cut me some more ear loops," she said. She watched as Lucinda measured and cut two pieces, then, sure Lucinda was doing it correctly, continued. "I left because I wanted to give Sylvia a chance to spend some time with you and your sister. And I knew this sewing machine was up here, waiting for me." She held out her hand. "Ear loops?"

Lucinda passed her the strips of elastic and watched Mom sandwich them between the fabric rectangles that used to be a dish towel. She started sewing again.

"What are you going to do with all these?"

"Hm?"

Lucinda raised her voice over the whir of the sewing machine. "The face masks. What are you going to do with them?"

"Oh, I thought I'd take them to give away at the farm stand," Mom said. "That way anybody who needs one can just . . . take one."

"So much work," Lucinda said. "Why not just buy them?"

Mom didn't say anything for a moment, and Lucinda wondered if maybe the sewing machine had drowned out her voice again. She was about to let it go, to move on to a new question, when Mom finally answered. "I don't know. I guess I've always just liked the idea of taking something that's old or torn or maybe not working the way it's supposed to anymore and making it new again. It makes me feel like there's *something* I can do, even if I can't fix it, you know?"

Lucinda wasn't sure she did know. But she nodded anyway. She would think about it. For now, she thumbed through the thick stack of fabric that sat at the edge of the table. She recognized not just the dish towels, but leftover scraps from projects Mom had made back at home, and even some of the clothes she and Raquel had outgrown. All waiting to be turned into something new.

"Looking for Sylvia's laundry?" Mom asked. Her eyebrow was arched, and Lucinda felt her cheeks go warm. "Over there," Mom said, raising her chin toward the living room. "On the bookshelf."

What had once been Sylvia's lucky leopard-print blouse was now a face mask with three sharp pleats. Lucinda traced her fingers over the straight white stitches.

"You can take it to her when you go back to the house," Mom said.

There was one more question Lucinda had to ask, even though she thought she knew the answer, and even though she didn't like it.

"Are you really going back home?"

Mom stopped the sewing machine. "I really am," she said. "I need to check on Mrs. Moreno, and the apartment. And I have some more salon deliveries to make. But I'll stay until Monday, just to be extra sure you're all settled. After that, I'll come back every weekend until this is over. And, Lu, I promise, it *will* be over someday."

Sometimes it was hard to believe that was true. But she decided to try.

She found Dad, Sylvia, and Juliette still on the patio, talking under the twinkling lights that Dad had strung up last summer. Seeing them sitting there together, she thought about her family and whether they could stitch all the pieces together into something new. She thought about Raquel and what they had outgrown, but also about what still fit.

"I'll be back in a sec," Lucinda said. She was hoping she could convince Raquel to join them. And maybe they could give Sylvia the face mask together. But when she got to the back door, she froze. Her throat tightened. The door was swinging open.

"Crybaby?"

24

"Um . . . What exactly are you looking for?"

Raquel pulled her head out from under the bed and unmuted herself to answer Daisy.

After Sylvia left, she had taken the laptop to her bedroom and called another emergency meeting. Not everyone could join, but Daisy was there. So were Alice, Peter, and Olivia. Raquel had filled them in on what happened at dinner and what Sylvia said about never wanting to leave.

"Sorry," Raquel said. "It's . . . my sister's cat. I saw him a minute ago and just wanted to make sure he was still in here."

"Crybaby!" Daisy squealed. "Bring him out! I want to say hello to that sweet, handsome boy!"

"Bring him out" was exactly what Raquel was trying to do, except Crybaby wasn't where he was supposed to be.

"I'm . . . sure he's around here somewhere," Raquel said. "Let's keep going. How are we going to get rid of Sylvia? What other ideas do you have?"

They all looked away from their cameras.

"Anyone?" Raquel asked.

"Oh, I know!" Daisy said. "What if you program her phone so the alarm goes off every twenty minutes tonight? If that doesn't drive Sylvia away, at least she'll be too tired and cranky to spend any time with your dad tomorrow."

That's when Raquel heard Lu's voice at the back door. "Crybaby?"

"Hang on," she interrupted Daisy. "Maybe we don't need a new plan after all."

If everything worked the way Raquel thought it might,

Lu would panic after seeing the back door that *Sylvia* had so thoughtlessly left open.

But Raquel wouldn't let her worry for too long. Miraculously, she would discover Crybaby under the bed—or wherever he was hiding now. It would have been a close call, but if anything *had* happened to Crybaby, Sylvia would be the one to blame. Maybe it wasn't enough to convince Dad that bringing Sylvia here was a mistake. But it might be exactly what she needed to get Lu back on her side again.

She just had to find Crybaby.

"What's going on?" Olivia asked.

"Yeah," said Alice. "Is everything all right?"

"Everything's fine," Raquel said as she scanned the room. "Just looking for that cat." The closet. *Of course!* She should've checked there first. Lately Crybaby liked to curl up in the corner and rest on top of the comic book boxes.

But he wasn't in the closet, either.

Lu and the rest of them were in the kitchen now.

"Calma, mija, I'm sure he's in here somewhere," Dad

was saying. "The door can't have been open for very long."

"I was *sure* I had closed it," Sylvia said. "I'll never forgive myself if anything . . . Marcos, where do you keep the flashlights?"

"Maybe he's with Raquel," Juliette suggested.

Raquel checked inside Lu's laundry basket and underneath the dresser. "I would have noticed if he left the room," she muttered to herself. *But maybe not if I was too focused on splitting up Dad and Sylvia to pay attention.*

Lu's footsteps thudded down the hall. "Crybaby? Are you in there?"

"Was that Lucinda?" Peter asked. "What's happening? She sounds upset."

"Gotta go," Raquel said to the screen, thoughts racing. "I'll explain everything on the group chat."

Mom raced over from the loft as soon as Dad called to tell her what happened. She had already changed into the sweatpants and the old concert T-shirt that she usually slept in, Raquel noticed. Which made her feel even worse.

Knowing she caused the kind of emergency Mom would bolt out of bed for.

Lu was sitting on the sofa, her face all wet and pink and blotchy. Mom held both her hands.

"He couldn't have gone very far," she said. "I'm sure he'll come straight home as soon as he's hungry. Just like when he sneaks downstairs to visit Mrs. Moreno."

Raquel's phone pinged again. It hadn't stopped since she sent that message to the group chat. She got up off the carpet and drifted into the kitchen to look at the screen.

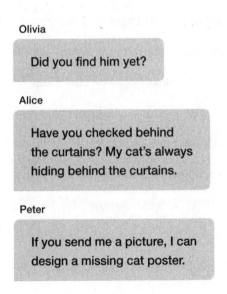

Olivia

Did you find him yet?

Alice

Have you checked behind the curtains? My cat's always hiding behind the curtains.

Peter

If you send me a picture, I can design a missing cat poster.

Raquel put the phone back in her pocket.

More tears streamed down Lu's cheek. "But what about the coyotes? You said there are coyotes."

Mom pressed her lips together and stroked Lu's hair. "Your dad and Sylvia are looking for him."

She didn't say they'd find him, though.

I should have closed the door. Raquel thought again. It was a thought that had crowded out all the other ones since she realized Crybaby was really missing. *I should have closed the door* and *I should have known this was going to happen.*

She couldn't stand to just sit there any longer. "I want to go out and look for him, too. Dad and Sylvia are searching the orange grove. I can go check the cherries."

Mom glanced out the window. "I know you want to help, mi amor, but it's too dark out there."

Juliette, who had been sitting at the kitchen table, so quietly that Raquel almost forgot she was there, spoke up.

"What if we go out together?" she said. "Me and Raquel?"

Mom bit her bottom lip, thinking about it.

Raquel didn't want to go with Juliette. She wanted to find Crybaby on her own, and then she wanted to stay up late, whispering and laughing with Lu. Just Lu. But if letting Juliette tag along convinced Mom to let her search, she wouldn't argue.

"Please, Mom?"

"All right. But stay together."

Once outside, Raquel checked her phone again and groaned as she scrolled through the messages.

Olivia

> No offense, Raquel, but I think you should have closed that door. #TeamSylvia

Daisy

> But Sylvia's the one who left the door open in the first place. She should have been more careful. #TeamAndrea

"On the track team, we call that a text avalanche," Juliette said.

Raquel jumped. "What?"

"Sorry. I didn't mean to startle you. I was just saying, we call that a text avalanche. You know, when one person sends something and everyone has to respond, and the messages come pouring in faster than you can keep up with them."

Track team was *nothing* like newspaper club. "It's not like that." Raquel silenced her phone and tapped on the screen to turn on its flashlight. "Anyway, I just want to focus on finding Crybaby, if you don't mind. And it was nice of you to offer to help and everything, but I can do it myself. Lu is *my* sister, after all."

Juliette jogged out ahead of her. "I wanted to help. I've never seen Lu so upset, and I'm good with animals." She shined her flashlight down the first row of cherry trees.

"Of course you haven't seen her upset. You barely know her. And how can you be good with animals? You don't have any pets . . . do you?"

Juliette trudged farther down the row, hopping over a hose. "Not exactly. Our landlord doesn't allow them, so Mom signed us up to volunteer at the animal shelter. We used to go every Saturday before, you know, *all this*."

"That's kind of . . . cool, actually," Raquel said. Although she had a hard time picturing Sylvia in an animal shelter.

"I know. And Mom makes these adorable videos of the dogs and cats, to help them get adopted. I was telling Lucinda about it. You should check them out sometime."

There was a rustling in the tree behind them. They spun around and pointed their flashlights in the branches.

"Crybaby?" Raquel called.

But it was only a squirrel.

She turned in a slow circle, trying to force her eyes to see farther into the darkness. "It's too big," she said, more to herself than to Juliette. "We're never going to find him, are we?"

"Let's keep looking," Juliette said, and turned to walk down another row of trees.

Raquel had left her notebook behind in the bedroom, but she made a mental picture of it now. She imagined writing down the facts she had gathered so far about Sylvia.

1. She drives a red car and wears leopard-print shirts, neither of which belongs on a ranch.

2. She likes recipes that need special pots and pans to cook them.

3. She makes videos as her job and also, apparently, in her spare time.

4. She has a daughter the same age as me and Lu.

5. She isn't Mom.

Some of the facts were more annoying than others. But even Raquel could admit there weren't enough of them yet to tell the whole story. If one of her staffers turned in an article like that, with so many holes in it, she'd ask them to go back and find out more.

"Wait, did you hear that?" Juliette held up her hand to signal that they should stop walking.

"Probably just an owl," Raquel said. "They live in the oak trees."

"No," Juliette said. "Listen. Over there!"

She took off toward the center of the orchard. Raquel ran after her, and as they got closer, she heard it, too.

Meee-ooowoar.

"That's him!"

Juliette got to the tree before she did. She aimed her flashlight up into the branches, and Crybaby's eyes glowed back at them.

Meee-ooow, he whined again.

Raquel staggered backward and let out a small, shaky laugh. "There you are!" She tossed her phone to Juliette. "Hold this for me. I'm gonna go get him."

Crybaby was perched on a thin branch about halfway up the tree. Every time he moved a cautious paw to climb back down, the branch would shake and he'd cry and cling again.

"Don't worry," Raquel said. "I'm coming!" She wedged her foot into a fork near the bottom of the trunk and pulled herself up. Lu would have been faster, she knew as she squinted to find another toehold. Lu would have known where to move next. But, slowly, Raquel climbed until, hugging the trunk with one arm, she could reach out with the other and pull Crybaby into her chest. "Gotcha."

He purred loudly as she cradled him in the crook of her elbow and made her way back down the tree.

"Look who I found," Raquel said, leaping off the last branch.

But Juliette wasn't there.

Raquel's cell phone lay blinking in the dirt. Messages flashed on the screen.

#TeamSylvia

#TeamAndrea

25

Crybaby spent the whole night curled on Lucinda's pillow, and the next morning, he dozed in her lap, stretching his neck every few minutes to remind her to keep scratching behind his ears.

"I don't think I have ever seen a more spoiled gato," Mom said as she stirred a splash of creamer into her coffee. She joined them for breakfast, just like she had promised, and Lucinda wondered how many alarms she had to set to wake up on time.

"I think he ran away on purpose," Dad said. "Just for the attention."

That made Sylvia bury her face in her hands. "I can't tell you how sorry I am for letting him get out," she said. It was at least her fifth apology that morning. "I don't know where my head was at, but I can promise you it won't happen again," Sylvia said.

"No harm done, Sylvia," Mom said. "Really. It was an accident. Anyone could have made the same mistake."

But Sylvia's the only one who did, Lucinda thought. Maybe Raquel was right all along. She shouldn't have trusted Sylvia so easily.

In all the commotion of the night before, she hadn't had a chance to thank her sister. Or even to hear exactly what had happened out in the cherry orchard.

She and Mom had been scouring the pantry for a can of tuna they could use to lure Crybaby back to the house when Jules charged through the back door. "We found him," she said as she stalked across the kitchen. But she didn't explain. Or even say another word. She just marched straight to her bedroom.

Raquel came in minutes later, carrying Crybaby. He wriggled out of her arms and galloped toward Lucinda, who had dropped to her knees to pick him up. "Where was he?" she had asked.

"Stuck in one of the cherry trees." Lu expected her to tell them more, to fly into the whole story as usual. But all Raquel said was "He must have climbed up too high and couldn't figure out a way down again." And Lucinda was so happy to have Crybaby back in her arms that she didn't think to ask more questions, or to wonder why her normally chatty sister seemed so quiet.

Now she wondered. She tried to get her attention, but Raquel's eyes stayed glued to the strawberry-quinoa breakfast bowl, not even nibbled, that Sylvia had put in front of her.

Sylvia looked down at her watch. "It's not like Juliette to oversleep," she said. "She must be tired after all the excitement last night. I'd better go wake her so she can get ready for school."

Raquel's head popped up. "Hey, Mom, maybe Lu and I should do school in the loft. That way Jules will have the place to herself. We won't disturb her."

Mom swallowed one last gulp of coffee. "All of your books and things are here," she said. "Besides, I have a big day of sewing planned."

"And besides *again*," Sylvia added, "Jules is going to be so happy to finally have some company, even if you're technically going to two different schools."

Even after two months, Lucinda thought, it was strange to think about how people could be in the same place together, but also not.

Mom yawned and brought her mug to the sink. She rinsed it out and turned it upside down on the drying rack. Then she came back to the table and kissed the top of Lucinda's head and walked around to the other side to kiss Raquel's. Just as if they were really going off to school.

"You two come see me at lunchtime, okay?" she said. She started for the back door just as Jules walked in from the hallway. They all turned around.

"There you are! I was just about to go wake you," Sylvia said. Her smile melted like the crayons Raquel and Lucinda had left out on the balcony once.

Jules was wearing a new DIY T-shirt. This one was white with iron-on letters that spelled out #TeamSylvia.

Lucinda dropped her spoon. It hit the edge of her bowl with a noisy clang that frightened Crybaby off her lap. How could Jules have known about Team Sylvia? Panicked, she looked across the table at Raquel. Her sister's shoulders tensed. She was crumpling her napkin into a tiny ball.

"Good morning, everyone!" Jules said. It was like she had walked in with venomous snake around her neck and everyone could see it but her. "Ooh! Quinoa-strawberry. Nice!" She served herself a bowl and sat down.

Sylvia laughed nervously. "Jules, honey, what are you wearing?"

Jules swallowed and looked down. "This? You should probably ask Lucinda and Raquel about it." She took another bite. Chewed. Swallowed. "Oh, and ask them to tell you about how they turned our lives into some weird reality-show dating competition for their friends. Are you Team Sylvia or Team Andrea? I think we all know whose side I'm on. Is there any more fresh orange juice?"

Mom took her hand off the doorknob and walked slowly back toward the kitchen table. "Lucinda, Raquel, what's going on?"

Lucinda's mouth was too dry to speak. "It's . . . We . . ."

"It's nothing," Raquel said, coming to her rescue like always. "Just a little inside joke that got *slightly* out of hand, that's all. And anyway, *she* was in on it, too!" She pointed at Jules. "Don't you remember? You wanted to leave as much as we wanted you gone!"

"Raquel!" Dad said.

Sylvia put her hand on Jules's shoulder. "You need to tell me what this is about."

Jules ignored her. "I wanted to go home," she shouted at Raquel. "But I didn't want you to sabotage my mom's relationship!"

She looked up at Sylvia. "*She* was the one who ruined your cake. And I *knew* the face mask thing wasn't just some misunderstanding. Oh, and here's the best part: She's *also* the one who let Crybaby out. To frame you."

Out on the ice, Lucinda always knew, a split second before it happened, that she was about to fall. Her toe would catch at exactly the wrong moment, or her weight would shift too far to one side, and it didn't matter how hard she fought to stay upright, she was going to tumble.

She felt like that now.

She hadn't looked at her phone since the night before. She had been too worried about Crybaby to even think about it. And after Raquel brought him home, she was too tired and relieved. It was still sitting on the coffee table, in fact. Silently, she slid out of her chair to go get it.

Raquel leaped to her feet. "That's not true. Sylvia left the door open. She even admitted it."

There were dozens of unread messages. Lucinda's hands shook as she scrolled through them. Mom snatched the phone away before she could finish, but Lucinda had seen enough.

A lot of times at the rink there was someone nearby to help you back up when you fell. But other times, you had to shake off the ice and stand on your own.

She should have seen this coming. Lucinda looked straight at Raquel. "I don't know why I listened to you. You think you know what's best for everyone. You think you can control everything. But you don't and you can't."

26

If someone had walked into the kitchen just five minutes later, they probably wouldn't have known that anything out of the ordinary had happened. Sylvia left, saying she needed some air, and Juliette stormed back to her bedroom, where Raquel guessed she was logging in for school, same as they were about to do. Shaking his head and pulling on his baseball cap, Dad went out to work in the cherry orchard. Not even Mom stayed behind. She headed back to the loft after warning them that they'd talk about it all later.

Raquel and Lu sat side by side at the kitchen table. Like always. But not.

"We should probably sign in now," Lu mumbled, clicking the Join button. Their faces appeared next to the eighteen others that were already on-screen, stacked in little rectangle-shaped windows.

Sometimes, when her mind wandered in class, Raquel would imagine what might be happening just outside the frame, where she couldn't see. Like, was Peter's grandma keeping more than just cockatiels in her apartment? Or, what exactly were Alice's little brothers up to that made them shriek and holler all day?

And sometimes she wondered what everyone else was imagining about her and Lu.

That morning, at least, she had a pretty good idea.

The first private message came right as Ms. King was welcoming everyone to class.

So what happened when you brought Crybaby home?

"Ignore it," Lu muttered. Raquel closed the chat box.

But another message flashed on the screen right after the first.

Is Sylvia still there?

Raquel pulled the computer toward her.

Not now.

Do you mean she's not there right now? Or you can't talk about it right now?

Lu groaned and reached for the keyboard.

BOTH!

Not even that stopped them.

After a while, Raquel raised her hand. She knew the questions would keep coming. And anyway, it was going to be impossible to steer her thoughts toward trade in the ancient Nile Valley the way Ms. King wanted her to.

"Yes, Raquel?" Ms. King called on her. "Would you like to unmute and give us one example of how trade helped the Egyptian civilization continue to advance?"

She swallowed. "Oh. No, actually, I was just raising my hand because I'm starting to get a headache. I think it's from all this screen time?"

Ms. King frowned and leaned close to the screen. Her eyes darted right and left as if she was trying to peer into the little window that belonged to Lu and Raquel. But of course she couldn't.

"Are you okay?" she asked. "Is one of your parents nearby to help?"

"I'm fine," Raquel added quickly, recognizing the look that grown-ups seemed to get anytime one of them coughed or sneezed lately. "I think I just need a break, if that's all right?"

"All right," Ms. King said after a pause. "Lucinda, you'll make sure to let me know how your sister is doing?"

Lu nodded, and Ms. King went on with class. "Someone else. What are some of the ways trade influenced Egyptian civilization? Mira?"

Lu switched off the camera even though teachers were always asking them not to. For Lu to break a rule like that, even a little rule that didn't make much sense as far as Raquel could see, she must be really concerned. And if she was really concerned, then it was possible she wouldn't stay angry forever. Raquel felt a tug at her chest. Like maybe the cord that connected them hadn't snapped after all.

"What's the matter? Are you actually sick?"

Raquel shook her head.

Lu narrowed her eyes. "You're not going to try to make Mom and Dad *think* you're sick, are you?"

"No!" Raquel shouted. Then she forced herself to gulp down her frustration. "No. I just want to be outside for a while. Take notes for me?"

"Yeah."

"I'm sorry about Crybaby," she added, even though the words felt thick in her mouth. "And . . . all of it."

"I know."

April sunshine flitted through the cherry blossoms, splashing the sandy soil with light. For once, Raquel didn't have a plan. She had no idea where she would go, or what she would do. And her first thought when she spotted Dad inspecting leaves in the orchard was to turn on her heel and go someplace else.

But it was too late. He had spotted her, too.

"Raquel, ven acá."

She stopped. "I know you're mad at me, and I know I'm supposed to be in class right now, but I couldn't concentrate and I just thought—"

"Help me out with something, will you?" he interrupted.

"*Okaaay*." Raquel took a cautious step toward him. "With what?"

He beckoned her closer. "Checking for aphids. Come see."

Dad pulled on a branch to draw it lower. He examined the shoots and then the undersides of the leaves. Raquel stood on tiptoe to see over his arm.

"Sometimes you find the bugs," he said. "But if the leaves are curled or yellow, those can be signs, too. This one looks all right." The branch sprang back up as he let it go.

"How many do you have to check?" Raquel asked.

"Oh," Dad said, and she followed his gaze as it swept the orchard. "All of them."

They got to work, leapfrogging each other down the row of trees. At first, Raquel expected he would want to talk to her about Mom or about Sylvia or about all the other secrets he might suspect she still was keeping. But he didn't. He didn't say anything. And as she examined the leaves—each one a question she could ask and answer and then let go—she felt her thoughts still and her shoulders relax for the first time since anyone mentioned symptoms and studies and curfews and quarantines.

"Mom would have let us come anyway," she said, surprising herself because she hadn't meant to say it aloud. Although she wasn't sorry she had.

"¿Mande?"

"Mom would have let us come stay here. On our own, I mean. I made Lu tell you she wouldn't let us come without her. But that wasn't true."

Dad chuckled.

Raquel let go of the branch she was inspecting and put her hands on her hips. "You already knew?"

"Mija," Dad said, "Your mother and I speak almost every day. Who did you think you were fooling?"

"You do?" She moved on to the next tree. "Then why did you go along with it?"

"We knew it would be hard. But we also knew it was important to you. So we made a decision to grow through it. Together. Same as we grow through everything."

Not long after, they made it to the end of the row. Dad went inside for lunch, but Raquel wasn't ready. She sat in the dirt, leaning against a tree trunk, and turned on her phone. Ignoring all the text messages, she clicked on the camera library and scrolled through the photos and videos she had taken over the past two months. The empty shelves at the grocery store. The computer screen during the *Manzanita Mirror*'s very first virtual staff meeting. Mom and Lu in the vegetable patch. Their collection of upcycled face masks. Juliette on her Rollerblades. Sylvia's face when she tasted the garlic on her orange cake.

She put the phone back in her pocket and thought about all the pictures that were missing. Of the school play and the chess tournament and the basketball championship and the book fair. Of Juliette's track meet and Lucinda's skating competition. No one knew how long All This would last or what would happen next. They could only grow through it together.

Finally, Raquel heard what she had been waiting for: Sylvia's footsteps on the gravel driveway. She ran out to meet her.

"You came back," she said.

Sylvia tilted her head. "Of course I did. Did you think I wouldn't?"

Raquel didn't answer right away. She looked over Sylvia's shoulder, past the gates, and out toward the highway and all the places Sylvia could've gone that weren't back home.

"No. I knew you would." She had to come back for Jules, of course. But Raquel knew there was more to it than that. "You seem kind of stubborn."

Sylvia smiled. "When I really care about something, yes. You're the same way, I think."

Raquel let her chin drop to her chest. "I'm sorry I tried

to sabotage everything. I should've given you a chance. Like Lu said."

"I think I understand why you did it," Sylvia answered. "And I'm sorry, too." Raquel looked up. It wasn't what she was expecting to hear. Sylvia reached for one of the cherry branches and ran her fingers over the pink blossoms. "I was just so set on making this plan of ours work that I didn't stop to think about how much change you've already been through. We should have given you more time to adjust."

"It's just that you were never part of *our* plan," Raquel said.

A few of the petals fluttered down, and one landed on Raquel's shoulder. Sylvia brushed it off. "I had convinced myself that the three of you girls would be just as excited as I was to be a part of a bigger family. Do you think, maybe, we can have a do-over?" she asked.

"No such thing as do-overs," Raquel said. "Sometimes I wish there was, but I don't think that's how it works. We can keep trying, though. And since you're planning to stick around, maybe you can help me with a new project?"

27

Lucinda wasn't expecting to bump into Juliette when she went out for a run on Saturday, just after breakfast in the loft. But she wasn't surprised, either. All she wanted that morning was to do something that felt *usual* the way her training routine felt usual. That's probably what Jules wanted, too.

She found her in the vegetable patch. Lucinda stopped to watch as Jules sprinted between two rows of garlic. She sped up faster, arms pumping at her sides, until she came to a line drawn in the dirt, pushed off her left foot, and leaped. Jules seemed to float a moment before landing on her heels, far from where she had taken off.

"That was amazing," Lucinda said, even though she hadn't planned to say anything at all. "I wish I could jump like that."

Jules looked up from the ground and frowned. "Don't you and your sister have any more relationships to wreck?" she said. "Do you really have to come out here and interrupt my practice?"

Now Lucinda wished she had just kept on jogging. But she knew she owed Jules an explanation. And an apology.

"I'm sorry," she said. She walked over to where Jules was sitting and offered her an arm. Jules took it and pulled herself up. "We got carried away, I guess. And . . . It's hard to explain. We didn't want to lose our dad."

Jules dusted off her hands. She pulled a measuring tape out of her pocket and handed one end to Lucinda. "Hold this for me?"

Then she pulled the other end out and walked it over to the line in the dirt.

"It's always been just Mom and me," Jules went on. "She said living with you two would be kind of like having a team. We might not be exactly the same, and we might not get along all the time, but we would have each other's backs. I should've known it was going to be two-on-one."

It reminded Lucinda of something Mom had said the night before in the loft. Lucinda and Raquel spent the night there to talk—and to give everyone some space. What they had gotten so wrong, Mom told them, was that there was never a Team Andrea *or* a Team Sylvia. They were all on the same side, cheering the girls on.

Lucinda and Jules lowered the measuring tape to the ground.

"It's not two-on-one," Lucinda said. But they weren't exactly a team yet, either. "We could try being like . . . workout partners, maybe?" They could practice a little every day. They could help one another get stronger.

Jules raised her eyes to the sky. She tapped her finger against her lips. "Hmmm . . . All right. It's a deal." She smiled. "If I'm gonna be stuck with you two, I think I want you on my side." Then she looked down at the measuring tape. Her shoulders dropped. "Thirteen feet, nine inches."

"That's not good?"

"It's not even a personal best, and I'm trying to beat the school record, fourteen feet. Not that it matters since all the meets are canceled."

Lucinda hesitated. She didn't know anything about track and field, but there was something she did notice earlier about Jules's jump.

"Don't get mad," she said, letting go of the measuring tape and watching it zip back into its case. "But speaking as your workout partner, maybe it would help if you kept your head up when you go into the jump."

Jules didn't respond. Lucinda tilted her chin to demonstrate. "*Up*. Like this?"

Still, Jules just stared. "I don't know," Lucinda added quickly. "It's this thing my skating coach is always telling me, so I thought—"

"My head was totally up!" Jules said.

Lucinda shook her head. "Nope. Sorry. You were definitely looking down."

"No way."

Lucinda pulled her phone from her waistband. "Do it again, just like you did before, and I'll record you."

Jules jogged over to her starting place, and Lucinda backed up out of the way. She got her camera ready. "Go!"

Once again, Jules bolted between the garlic rows and jumped. And once again, her head dipped as she came to the line in the dirt.

Lucinda replayed the video and froze it right as Jules was taking off. "Okay, come look!" Jules peered over her shoulder.

"Look at what?" It was Raquel. Lucinda hadn't noticed her walking over from the orange grove and suddenly felt caught between Jules and her sister again. Was Jules still angry? Would Raquel resent that Lucinda was spending time with her? Maybe. But then she remembered, *same side*.

"Raquel!" she said, waving her over. "Look at this." Raquel stood next to her but covered the screen with her hand before Lucinda could press Play.

"Wait, first, I have to say something," she started.

"What? That you're sorry for being such a jerk?" Juliette asked. "I know. And I'll let it slide. But just this once."

"Really?"

Juliette shrugged. "I might have tried to scare Marcos off when they first started seeing each other. But they seem pretty determined."

"Really?" Raquel said again, less surprised this time and more like she wanted to be let in on a secret.

This was getting dangerous. Lucinda cleared her throat. "Now that we're all settled, can we please get back to the video?" She tapped the screen. "Now, Kel, tell me what you notice about Jules's head. Just as she jumped."

"She looked down," Raquel said right away.

"UGH!" Jules groaned. "I *knew* it was going to be two-on-one." Only, this time she was laughing.

Lucinda laughed, too. "All right, do it again and this time, think, *Up!*"

Jules took off a third time. Lucinda watched her through the camera lens, whispering, "Up, up, up," as Jules thundered down the row.

This time when Jules sprang off the ground, she kept her chin tilted up, like an invisible string was pulling her forward.

She landed and looked over her shoulder. "I think that was farther!"

"Let's measure!" Lucinda said, grabbing the measuring tape from where they had dropped it in the dirt. She took one end. Raquel took the other.

"I don't want to know," Jules said, covering her ears.

Lucinda and Raquel looked at each other.

"Okay, I *do* want to know. What is it?" Jules held her breath.

"Wait!" Lucinda said. "Record it, Kel." She had a good feeling about this. She ran over to kneel beside Jules.

"All right." Raquel took out her phone and aimed it at the two of them as she announced, "Fourteen feet, one inch."

Jules and Lucinda screamed.

"You did it! You beat the record!"

"Too bad nobody saw," Jules said.

Raquel tapped on her phone screen to stop the recording. "*We* were here. We saw it."

28

Raquel texted Mom for the third time that morning. She knew she should have set more alarms.

> Where are you????
> It's almost time.

Mom

> On my way, Kel. But it's going to take me even longer if I have to keep replying to these messages!

It was Tuesday morning again. The *Manzanita Mirror*

hadn't posted late all year, and Raquel Mendoza did not intend to break her streak. Everything was ready. She had uploaded the last pictures the night before, Daisy and Lu proofread every page twice, and Ms. King gave her final approval to all the stories.

This is remarkable work, she wrote to the staff. *You all should be very proud of yourselves. You are writing the first draft of history!*

All Raquel had to do was hit Publish. She set the laptop at the center of the kitchen table and arranged the chairs so everyone would have a good view of the screen.

"Five minutes till we go live!" Sylvia sang out as she crossed the kitchen with a pitcher of juice, squeezed from oranges they picked that morning. Sylvia hadn't been able to sleep, either, so she and Raquel went out together, when the orchard was still moonlit, to pass the time while they waited for everyone else to wake up.

"Maybe you should go get her, Lu," Raquel said, stealing another nervous look at the clock. They had convinced Mom to stay in Lockeford an extra day so she would be there when the *Mirror* published, and now she was going to miss it. "Or, on second thought, maybe you, Jules. You run faster."

Lu nearly tripped over Crybaby, who was circling her feet, meowing. She picked him up. "Seriously, Raquel, no one's going to notice if it posts at 7:02 a.m."

"*I'll* notice!" What was the point of having a schedule if you didn't stick to it?

Jules yawned and leaned her head on Sylvia's shoulder.

"She said she'd be here by seven, mija," Dad said, ruffling Raquel's hair. "She'll be here."

Finally, the back door opened. "Good morning!" Mom's hair was still dripping from the shower, and she had one of Abuelita's hand-crocheted blankets wrapped over her shoulders.

Dad winked and went to pour Mom a cup of coffee. Sylvia pulled out the chair nearest the computer. "You sit up front, Andrea. You're not going to want to miss this."

Mom sat. "Thank you, I can't wait." Then she took

Raquel's hands and squeezed. "So, can we see your big surprise now?"

Raquel looked up at the clock again. "One more minute! Is everyone ready?"

They all sat behind her.

"Should we count down or something?" Jules asked.

"Don't give her any ideas," Lu said. "Or we'll have to do this *every* Tuesday morning."

Raquel ignored her. She watched the clock on the computer screen. When it changed to 7:00, she clicked the button that said Publish and let out a long, slow breath as the latest edition of the *Manzanita Mirror* appeared on-screen.

The heading on top read, "Apart from All This: A Special Edition of the *Manzanita Mirror*."

Underneath was an editor's note.

Instead of writing about our school this week, we decided to write about ourselves. That's because despite everything that's happening in the world, we're still learning and growing. Some of us are even making new friends.

And even though we have to stay far apart for now, we are finding ways to come together. This is one of them. We hope you enjoy it!

—Raquel Mendoza, Editor in Chief

The page was filled with stories from their classmates about what they missed most since the big All This had started. What they were looking forward to when it was over. What they would never forget.

Raquel had gotten the idea when she was working in the cherry orchard with Dad. Later that night, she sent one more urgent message to the newspaper club group text: *What if we postpone the articles we've been working on and make a special edition instead?*

She explained her idea then, and when they all agreed, she wrote, *Great! We only have three days. Tell everyone you know to send us their stories!*

And they had.

Obviously, I miss seeing my friends the most, but I also miss the cafeteria and how on baked potato days, Ms. Lizeth would always save the biggest one for me because she knows it's my favorite. Since my mom still has to work, my brother came home from college to watch the rest of us during the day. He's has to study, too, though, so all he has time to make for lunch is instant ramen. I'm so sick of instant ramen.

This might sound weird, but I really miss the sound of our classroom during silent reading time. How it's so quiet you can hear the clock ticking and the pages turning. You can even hear Mr. Lopez's pen when he's grading our assignments! It's quiet at my house, but it's not the same.

I can't wait to have birthday parties again. Mine was supposed to be back in March. We sent the invitations and bought all the decorations and everything. It was going to be neon-themed. Then all this happened, and we had to cancel it. My friends surprised me with a drive-by celebration, though. I never thought that waving at someone from the front lawn could feel like a real party, but it actually did!

I thought I was going to miss orchestra the most. I mean, how can you have an orchestra if no one is allowed to be in the same room together? Then, one day, we all got this email from Mrs. Lawrence, and it said, "Go look on your front porch!" So I did, and you're never going to believe this, but somehow Mrs. Lawrence had delivered each of us an ukulele from the school music room! I still want to go back to the clarinet, but I think I'll keep on playing ukulele, even when all this is over.

I don't even care anymore that we didn't get to finish the basketball season. Even though I was really mad about it at first because I was a starter this year, and I know we would have made it to the playoffs. I just want to practice with my team again.

Mom and Dad read through the stories. They laughed at some. They smiled sadly at others.

And they hadn't even gotten to the best part yet.

When she couldn't stand waiting any longer, Raquel pulled the computer toward her. "You guys are taking too long!" She found the video posted near the bottom of the page.

Sylvia, who was standing behind Dad the whole time, finally sank into her own chair. *"Thank you!* I thought they'd never get to it."

Raquel pressed Play.

The first clip was of Alice, in full costume and makeup, singing one of her big songs from *Xanadu Jr.*

Then came a clip of Nathan Burns, who demonstrated the remote-controlled rover he had been coding for the robotics challenge.

Then Charlie Lam and Maya Copeland, in side-by-side videos shot in their bedrooms, delivering the arguments they had prepared for speech and debate.

"It's everything we've been working on that we never got a chance to show off," Raquel explained. "Sylvia helped me edit it all together."

Mom looked over her shoulder at Sylvia and said, "Thank you." Then she turned back to Raquel. "This is amazing, Kel. You've turned all these little pieces into something really special."

Raquel pointed at the screen. "Look! You're going to miss it!"

It was Lu, wearing her skating dress and Sylvia's old Rollerblades, performing her competition program on the patio.

"When did you two do this?" Dad asked.

"Yesterday morning," Lu said. She got off her chair and twirled in time with her image on the screen. "While you were doing chores in the garden."

"Well, you'll have to give an encore performance," Dad said. "I need to see the live version."

Lu giggled. "Okay!"

The video faded to black, and Sylvia started clapping.

"Just wait," Raquel said. "Keep watching."

The video faded back in on Jules in the vegetable garden, getting ready to sprint between the rows of garlic.

"What's this?" Sylvia said, leaning forward. "You must have added it after we finished."

"Just wait," Lu and Raquel repeated.

Off-screen, Lu's voice in the video said, "GO!"

The six of them watched Jules take off running and heard Lu whisper, "Up, up, up." Then Jules leaped. She raised her arms above her head as she sailed forward and dropped them as she landed feetfirst in the dirt.

The next clip came from Raquel's camera. "Fourteen feet, one inch," her voice announced.

Sylvia screamed along with the video. She leaned over and threw her arms around Jules's neck. "Yes! You did it! I can't believe you didn't tell me!"

Jules waved her hands. Her eyes widened as the next clip, the last one, came into focus. "Mom! It's Coach Bradley! Look!"

A woman in a blue warm-up jacket appeared on-screen. There was a case full of trophies behind her.

"Hi, Jules," she said. "It's me, Coach Bradley. Your friend Raquel sent me the video of your long jump, and, wow, I can't tell you how proud I am. As you can see, I'm here in the athletics office. I came back just so I could enter your name in the official record book. Keep practicing, okay? I'll see you soon."

Then the video faded out for real.

No one spoke for a moment. Sylvia wiped a tear from the corner of her eye and said, "How did you do that?"

Raquel shrugged. "It wasn't hard. I remembered the name of the school from that sticker on the back of your car. Then I found the track coach's email on the school website."

Lu put her arm around her shoulder. "My sister always pays attention to the important details."

After that, it was almost time for school to start. Dad helped Mom pack up her car, and Lu went to the pantry to get her a jar of escabeche to take back to Mrs. Moreno and her grandson.

Mom kissed their foreheads and said she'd see them the next weekend.

"Can you bring more Corn Chex?" Raquel said. "I finished the box last night." They waved goodbye as her car rolled back down the gravel driveway and onto Highway 88.

Raquel still didn't think it was possible to know exactly the moment everything changed. The situation was always changing. And maybe there was no such thing as do-overs. But there were some moments you wanted to replay frame by frame. Moments that felt bigger than others. Moments that left you happy and hopeful, even if you still weren't sure what might happen next.

Acknowledgments

This book isn't really about a pandemic, but it was written during one. And I will always be grateful to teachers and coaches like Sandra Arana, Kat Butenschoen, Melissa Cash, Romel De Silva, Amie Hanrahan, Ellen Hoffman, Nic Jimenez, Cher Krayer, Keely Milliken, Emily Relph, Monica Richter, Emily Grace Tucker, Maureen Usle, and J'Marie Ventrella who helped us through with such compassion and humor.

Mil gracias to my agent, Jennifer Laughran; to the insightful and extraordinary Tiffany Colón; to the talented Xochitl Cornejo; and to everyone at Scholastic, especially Melissa Schirmer, Stephanie Yang, Taylan Salvati, and Jordin Streeter for the heart and creativity you brought to this book. What an honor to work with you.

And, as always, to David, Alice, and Soledad, thank you for being the best team I've ever been on.

About the Author

Jennifer Torres is the author of *Stef Soto, Taco Queen, The Fresh New Face of Griselda,* and other books for young readers. She writes stories about home, friendship, and unexpected courage inspired by her Mexican American heritage. Jennifer started her career as a newspaper reporter, and even though she writes fiction now, she hopes her stories still have some truth in them. She lives with her family in Southern California.